301.97

THE GOLDEN GIRL

Sarah had everything — wealth, social background, great beauty and magnetic charm, a loving family and many friends. She was a golden girl, indeed — and her heart was ruled by love and compassion for the lesser fortunate in life. Yet, when one man's happiness was at stake and she could prove the pure gold of her heart and character, she failed him — and herself — and many storms swept the sea of her life before she finally reached safe harbour . . .

PAULA LINDSAY

THE GOLDEN GIRL

Complete and Unabridged

LINFORD
Leicester

First published in Great Britain

First Linford Edition
published 1997

Copyright © 1963 by Paula Lindsay
All rights reserved

British Library CIP Data

Lindsay, Paula, *1933*–
    The golden girl.—Large print ed.—
    Linford romance library
    1. English fiction—20th century
    2. Large type books
    I. Title
    823.9′14 [F]

    ISBN 0–7089–7984–X

Published by
F. A. Thorpe (Publishing) Ltd.
Anstey, Leicestershire
Set by Words & Graphics Ltd.
Anstey, Leicestershire
Printed and bound in Great Britain by
T. J. Press (Padstow) Ltd., Padstow, Cornwall

This book is printed on acid-free paper

1

THE streets were shrouded in dim, yellow fog and few people were about on the damp and dreary night. A policeman walked down the street with his heavy, measured tread, illuminated for a brief moment by the light from a street lamp. Occasionally light swathed through the gloom from a window in one of the tall houses.

A car turned into the silent street and a boy of ten pressed his nose even closer to the window pane and said shrilly: "There's the doctor's car. Now we shall have another squalling brat in the house!" There was a world of contempt in his youthful voice.

His sister glanced up from the task of removing her doll's day clothes and arraying her in a nightgown. "Does he bring the baby with him?" she asked with a stirring of interest. "I wonder if he'd bring me a real baby. I love Amanda but she doesn't cry when I smack her and she doesn't laugh when I kiss her." She sighed over the unresponsive doll.

Thomas turned and stared at his sister. "Don't you know where babies come from?" he demanded with all the worldly wisdom of his superior years. "Of course the doctor doesn't bring it with him. It's here all the time. He just helps to make it born."

Louise looked up again and this time her small face was puckered with bewilderment. She stared at Thomas for a long time. Then she said: "Where is it then? I asked Nanny and she said the baby wasn't here yet and the doctor would bring it in his bag."

Thomas jeered: "Kid stuff. You're such a baby you'd believe anything." He turned back to the window and watched in some awe as the doctor stepped from the car, a tall man in sombre clothes and carrying a leather bag. He seemed to sense the child's gaze for he looked up and raised his hand in a brief salute. He knew the children well for he treated them for their childish ailments and had brought them into the world.

Louise scrambled to her feet and padded to her brother's side. "Tell me where the baby is," she pleaded, sensing that Thomas was in a difficult mood and it was likely that she'd never know the truth if he did not explain it now. She greatly admired the brother who knew so much and talked to the servants in the same arrogant way that their father used. Louise was a little afraid of the servants — but she was, after all, a very small girl. Thomas was very mature for his age. His father laughed at him and said that he was precocious — but there was a note of admiration and awe in his voice when he used the word.

Thomas looked down at her thoughtfully. She was only five years old and he knew a surge of protective affection.

He knew that his father would be angry if he found out that he had been listening to Nanny when she gossiped with Ada. Perhaps he had better pretend that he had only been teasing. He was not sure that the information he had gleaned was the truth — and yet in his boyish mind he knew that the fairy tales which Nanny told them could not possibly be true.

He put his arms about Louise. "It's in the bag that the doctor brings with him," he said reassuringly. "Soon someone will come to tell us that we've a new baby brother or sister."

She was not old enough to be disillusioned — let her believe the fairy tales for the time being. Nanny did not encourage questions. Babies were out of her province, was her frequent, snubbing reply. The doctor brought them in his black bag. Thomas had found Louise in tears one day and learned that she was afraid that the baby would suffocate. She had heard Ada telling Nanny about her sister's baby who had rolled on to its face and died for want of air. He had quickly reassured his sister.

Arrogant, vain and precocious, thinking himself too old to be still in Nanny's care and anxious for the day when he would go to his public school, he was a kind-hearted boy and devoted to his sister — and he felt it his duty to dry her tears, comfort her with a few well-chosen words and divert her with a gift of a picture book which he had outgrown . . .

Dr. Blake rang the bell and listened to its dull intonation within the house. The door opened and he was admitted by the respectful butler. As he went in, a door on the right opened and Harry Fallow came into the hall.

"There you are, Blake. I expected you before this." His voice held reproach.

Blake shook hands and apologised for his late arrival. "It's a miserable night," he explained. "The fog is very patchy and the traffic in a poor way."

"Come and have a drink. Expect

you could use one." Harry led the way into his study and crossed to the decanters.

"Mrs. Fallow . . . ?" Blake reminded him delicately as he took the glass of sherry.

Harry gestured briefly. "Mrs. Drew is with her — a very capable woman. You've time to enjoy that sherry, Blake."

"Well . . . good health, Fallow."

Harry grinned. "Meaning that you hope I'll live to have another dozen kids . . . after all, you earn a fat fee each time, don't you?" His smile took the sting from the words. He was a big man: tall, hearty with a stocky frame and a ruddy complexion. He was vaguely defined as 'something in the City'.

Blake liked him for all his seeming indifference to his wife's condition. He knew that beneath the hearty air was an acute anxiety, for Sarah Fallow was a delicate woman and the last child, born barely a year ago, had taken its toll of her health and strength. He had warned Fallow then that there should be no more children — but now, only thirteen months later, he was called to the house to assist another Fallow infant into the world. He drank his sherry and moved towards the door.

"Are you worried, Blake? She'll be all right, won't she?"

He paused by the door. "I warned you last time of the risk, Fallow. I'll do my best — but I advise you to keep your fingers crossed."

He closed the door on those ominous words and Harry sank into a chair and buried his face in his hands. He adored his wife and their marriage had been happy. He might not always be considerate but he had been a good husband to the best of his ability. He could not visualise a life without Sarah. Perhaps it had been foolish to risk another child — but she laughingly reminded him of their original plan to have four children and promised him that this would be the last. He determined now that it would be the last . . .

Sarah Fallow tossed and turned in the big bed, the long hair flowing over the pillows. The big room seemed dark and cold and she shivered.

Mrs. Drew bent over the bed. "Are you cold, madam?"

Sarah muttered. Then she said firmly: "Yes, I'm damnably cold! It's a terrible night — is that fog streaming through the window?"

"A real November pea-souper," the woman replied. She bathed Sarah's forehead and brushed back the strands of fine, pale hair. The violet shadows beneath her eyes emphasized her pallor and the blue eyes were dark with pain. Yet with the tightly-stretched skin over the bones of her face, the violet shadows and the pale lips, there was still evidence of her natural beauty.

"What a night to be born," Sarah murmured and caught her breath as pain engulfed her slight body. She bit her lips, determined on silence. She had never cried out for any of the children — a tribute to her courage for childbirth had never been easy for her. "And what a night to die . . . " she added tremulously.

Sarah knew that she was going to die. She had known even on the night when she had shared Harry's passion and felt certain that she would have another child. She had known with vivid clarity throughout the last nine months. She knew now that she would not live to see another dawn. Pain was her foremost consideration at that moment. She could think of nothing else. But it did not matter. She had done all her thinking and now she waited for death with the calm fortitude of her nature.

Blake entered the room and she turned her head. He went to the bed and looked down at her, his eyes anxious for the moment and then reassuring as her heavy lids were raised and he met the penetrating gaze of her blue eyes.

"Well, Mrs. Fallow," he said brightly.

"You're soon in need of my services. What is it to be this time — girl or boy?" He lifted her wrist and felt the faint thread of her pulse. Her wrist was very thin and her fingers sought his as though in need of a comforting clasp. His hand was cool and firm.

His question did not require an answer, she knew. She scanned his face as though seeking confirmation for her own certainty. Then she said slowly: "I won't be able to help much — do your best, won't you? And let me see my husband as soon as possible."

Her words were stilled by a gust of violent pain and she clung fiercely to his hand while her indomitable spirit refused to allow a sound to pass her lips.

He bent over her compassionately. "There's no reason on earth why you shouldn't give way," he said kindly. "I don't mind — and you'll feel better for it." She shook her head — and he smiled down at one of the bravest and certainly the most stubborn women he had ever known.

It was a long battle. It seemed an eternity to the protagonists but just before the dawn the thin pipe of an infant's wail pierced the room. Blake handed the child to the anxious Mrs. Drew and concentrated on Sarah's needs but his mouth was set grimly and his eyes were dark with defeat. He had done all he could but Sarah was already almost beyond his help.

She said feebly: "Harry?"

He put his mouth close to her ear for she was fast drifting into the darkness. "I'll send for him now."

"The baby?" It was a mere whisper but he was glad that she was conscious that her ordeal was over.

"A girl," he said. "With a fine pair of lungs."

A smile flickered across her face and was gone in a moment. Blake stepped to the door and opened it. A maid was hovering in the corridor, anxious for news. The house was ablaze with light and seething with activity for only the children were in bed that night.

"Fetch Mr. Fallow . . . and quickly!" There was the note of urgency in his voice.

The girl sped down the wide staircase and he went back to his patient. He sought that thready pulse and knew that as he counted the beats so he counted her life away.

Harry was by the bed in one swift movement, brushing Blake to one side. One glance at Sarah's face told him all he needed to know and he fell on to his knees by the bed, hot tears surging to his lids and streaming unchecked down his ashen cheeks.

Blake discreetly withdrew with a nod to Mrs. Drew to accompany him. She still held the baby which cried intermittently. She said in a low whisper: "Poor little thing! The Lord giveth and the Lord taketh away."

Her pious comment irritated him beyond measure and to conceal his annoyance he took the child from her arms and gave it a cursory examination. He felt mentally and physically exhausted. He knew that no amount of medical skill could have prevented Sarah's death — yet illogically he felt that he had failed her and himself this night.

The door opened abruptly and Harry came out of the room, his features composed, his eyes calm and dry. "My wife is dead," he said in a voice that was cold as death itself. He glanced at the white bundle in Blake's arms with a hurtful indifference. "Is that the child?"

"It's a girl," Blake said dully and stepped past him to enter the room . . .

Harry sat in the deep armchair, his chin resting on his hand, his eyes gazing into the bright flames of the fire but seeing nothing but the lovely face of the woman he had loved. He was numb with the sense of loss and felt that life would be empty indeed without Sarah.

There was a brief tap on the study

door and he muttered an admission. A few minutes later, he was aware of the dispassionate gaze of two bright eyes and he looked up to find Thomas studying him, his hands locked behind his back, his unruly curls falling about his intelligent forehead.

Study of a man grieving for his dead love, Thomas thought calmly but did not dare to voice his reflection. He noticed the air of dejection, the listless eyes, the lack of laughter about the mouth — and visualized how he could transport such a monument of grief to canvas. For Thomas was destined to be an artist and he knew it. He was most happy when he sat with pencil and block. He enjoyed drawing pictures on the window panes when they were damp with condensation and his picture books had been completely filled with his attempts to copy their artistic splendours. He was convinced that he would be a successful and famous artist one day and he had little patience with those who failed to appreciate his talent.

However, the present was with him and the future was a delightful thing to fill his dreams, waking and sleeping. So he composed his features, adopting an appropriately mournful expression and said heavily: "You sent for me, Daddy?"

"Did I?" Harry stared at him and then pulled himself to the present. "Yes, of course. Well, my boy — what are we going to do now?"

Thomas looked at his father and despised him. It was natural that he should be unhappy because Mother had died. But if he continued to wallow in self-pity and gloom, he would soon lack the sympathy of his friends. Far better if he was gay and laughing again then everyone would say: '*Poor Fallow . . . his wife's just died, you know but he shows a brave face to the world. One has to admire him, don't you know!*' And it was wrong for a man to ask his ten-year-old son for advice — he shouldn't expect to cast his problems and responsibilities on my shoulders, he thought resentfully. He had loved Mother and it was very sad that she had died. But life went on and one could not mourn for ever. Mother had been a lovely and lively person, always gay, always laughing, always tenderly affectionate. She wouldn't like to know that everyone was pulling long faces and wiping tears from their eyes. She wouldn't like to hear the servants sniffling over their interminable cups of tea and sympathizing with the 'poor little motherless mites.'

But he kept his mature and cynical thoughts to himself — and wondered briefly how long he would have to wait before he was old enough to speak his mind without bothering about good manners and respect.

He said dolefully, knowing that it was expected of him: "Won't Mother ever come back?" He knew, of course, that she would not. She was dead and buried under six feet of cold clay . . . he had heard Ada saying so to Nanny. It didn't sound a pleasant fate but Mother couldn't know about it . . .

"I'm afraid not, Thomas." Harry sighed. He did not understand this boy of his. He and Sarah had always been completely absorbed in each other. The children spent their days in the nursery or at school and he had seen little of them. With Thomas he particularly felt ill at ease. He felt that the boy's bright eyes pierced into his innermost thoughts and feelings. There were even occasions when he sensed a certain contempt in the boy's manner — contempt! He quickly dismissed the fantastic thought.

He studied the boy now. A good-looking child with his mop of blond curls and those intelligent blue eyes — of tall and slender build with a strange dignity about him. He strongly resembled his mother . . . and Harry looked away as grief overwhelmed him again.

Thomas turned away to leaf through

one of the books that lay on the table and Harry was grateful for that gesture of tact. He decided abruptly that it was time the boy went to a public school. To have him in the house, within sight and sound, would only serve as a constant reminder of Sarah.

He said quietly: "Thomas, you've been pestering me about a public school for some time. I've decided to send you to Wychwood in the New Year."

Thomas, with the realization of his ambition, felt a strange reluctance to leave his home and his sisters. He did not analyse his emotion but there swept through him the fear that his father, wrapped in his grief, would forget about the girls and they would need him to look after them.

"What about the girls, Daddy?" he asked impulsively.

Harry gave him a sharp, impatient glance. He had expected the boy to show some pleasure, to thank him . . . "They'll be in good hands. Nanny will take care of them. You needn't worry your head about your sisters, Thomas."

"And Sarah?" he asked, a little timidly.

Harry reared at the name. "What?" He leaped to his feet angrily. "Who named the child after her mother?" he demanded, almost beside himself with rage.

Thomas moved away in panic. "I don't know . . . Nanny calls her Sarah . . . "

Harry reached for the bell. The butler came in with his heavy, respectful tread. "Send for Mrs. Drew."

He paced the big room while he waited and Thomas, not having been sent away and yet feeling himself in the way, cowered in the window seat and drew pictures on the windows.

Mrs. Drew bustled in, her skirts rustling, her agitation at the peremptory summons very obvious. Harry rounded on her immediately. "Who authorized the naming of the baby, Mrs. Drew?"

The housekeeper looked frightened and certainly Harry Fallow's fury was to be feared because it was so seldom aroused. "Why, sir . . . I asked you what to name her and you said you didn't care . . . call her what I pleased. Well, it's a fine name, sir — her mother's name . . . " She stumbled and faded into silence.

"Exactly!" he said coldly. "Her mother's name . . . I won't have it. Change it, Mrs. Drew. Change it to anything but Sarah!"

"But, sir . . . "

"Change it!" he roared.

Thomas decided to interfere. "Unfortunately, that isn't possible, Daddy."

Harry swung on his heel to glare at the boy. "What . . . are you still here? What do you know about it? You know too damned much for your age, my lad!"

"The baby has been baptized, Daddy," Thomas told him, unimpressed by his father's anger.

"Is this true?" Harry demanded of

his housekeeper. But now he spoke more quietly.

"Dr. Blake thought it advisable . . . the child hasn't been very well, sir. He said to have her baptized but not to worry you with the arrangements . . . that he'd attend to everything. Mr. Carter came to the house for the baptism." She paused and then added uncertainly: "Sarah Jane, sir — after Mrs. Fallow and your mother."

Harry was dumbfounded. "Where the devil was I while this was going on?"

"You went to the funeral, Daddy."

Harry turned on him swiftly. "Go to your room — and learn to keep a still tongue in your head!"

He went to the door. Then he paused and said reassuringly: "Never mind, Daddy. We'll call her Sally. I think that's a very pretty name." He closed the door softly behind him and ran up to the nursery, oblivious to his father's renewed anger which he expended on the unhappy Mrs. Drew.

Louise ran to him as he entered the nursery. "Come and see Sarah having her bottle," she said excitedly.

In a lordly manner, he said firmly: "Daddy and I have decided that she will be called Sally in future. And I'm going away to school after Christmas."

Her lower lip drooped and tears welled in her eyes. "What about me?" she wailed.

He put an arm about her small shoulders. "Oh, you'll be all right," he said with masculine confidence. "I'm leaving you in charge of Sally . . . you said you'd rather have a real baby to look after than that silly doll."

She wrenched herself away and ran to pick Amanda from the floor, forgetting her disdainful abandon of the doll a few minutes before. She hugged the doll and plastered the inscrutable china face with kisses. "I hope she didn't hear you," she wailed anxiously. "She can't help it if she's not . . . real." She dropped her voice to a whisper on the last word for she was still not quite sure that the doll didn't have a life of its own despite her inanimacy.

"Oh, come on . . . let's go and see Sally, Lulu."

She went with him because he rarely used the pet name she had devised for herself when she was first beginning to talk. He only used it when he was in an affectionate mood. She could not visualize a future without him and although he often annoyed or teased her or talked of things she did not understand, she felt in her childish way that life would never be the same again once Thomas went away to school.

He had always been a part of her life and no one would ever answer all her questions as Thomas did. Nanny usually brushed them off with '*ask no questions, you'll be told no lies*' or '*curiosity killed the cat*'. Louise did not know why lies should be the only answer to questions — and as for the cat, she felt sorry but she'd never had any curiosity so it wasn't likely to harm her. Sometimes she wondered if it was something to eat . . .

They went into the adjoining room and found Nanny sitting by the fire with the baby on her lap. She had been fed and changed and Nanny, a firm believer in exercise, was allowing her a few minutes kicking time. The baby was small but strong and there was the hint of future chubbiness in the small face and sturdy limbs.

"I thought you were with your Daddy," the ample, motherly woman said as Thomas entered.

"Well, I'm not," he said, almost rudely. "Has she finished her bottle!" he exclaimed in disappointment. "I wanted to feed her!" He touched the baby's smooth cheek with his finger. "Pretty Sally."

"Sally! Why, there's a fine thing to call your little sister. She has a lovely name, Thomas, and we don't want it distorted, thank you!"

He tossed his curls arrogantly. "My father and I have decided that she shall be called Sally."

"You mean your Daddy has decided," she amended. "Well, I can't say I'm surprised because I'm not."

"I'm hungry," Thomas complained. "It must be time for tea, Nanny — ring the bell!"

"Don't you give me orders, Thomas," she returned sharply. In the normal way of things, she doted on Thomas and denied him nothing. Usually she would laugh and obey his orders but today she resented it and her tone was cutting. He merely grinned and wandered back into the other room where he picked up Louise's slate and a blue crayon and endeavoured to portray his father — with bowed head wallowing in grief.

Some time later, Nanny came to call him to his tea and looked over his shoulder. She uttered a sharp exclamation of protest and wrenched the slate from his hands.

"You unfeeling child!" she snapped, rubbing at the slate with the corner of her apron.

His expression was oddly triumphant. "Did you understand it then, Nanny?"

She moved away from him as though she was disturbed by his precocity. "Of course," she muttered. "It was your poor Daddy crying over your Mother — and you're a very naughty boy to draw such things!"

Her words skated over his head. He was only thinking that at last someone had taken enough interest in his preoccupation with slate and crayon to notice — and it was the first time that his drawings had been recognizable to other than himself. They were oddly mature for a boy of his age — oddly abstract. The drawing of his father had been mere lines with no distinctive features — and he knew a strange sense of power for he realized that one day he would be acclaimed for his ability to transfer his ideas to the imagination of others . . .

Christmas came and Harry regained some of his former spirits. At first, he had felt that he did not welcome the festivities but he could not deny the children their right to the joys of the season and he could not help a feeling of excited anticipation as the holiday drew near. He found himself occasionally striding into the house with a jovial comment to old Standish on the icy roads or the state of the weather. He returned the hearty greetings of his business associates or social acquaintances with equal heartiness — until he remembered his bereavement and quickly lowered his tones to a mere nuance above graveside accents. He even accompanied an old friend to the theatre on Christmas Eve — and enjoyed himself with gusto until the formal acknowledgement of one of Sarah's relatives reminded him forcibly of his widower status.

In his oddly mature way, Thomas had hit the nail on the head. Fallow's friends did consider that Harry was showing a brave face to the world. They openly commented on his admirable restraint. He merited their sympathy because of his lack of sombre mourning — Harry hated black and after the first weeks reverted to the light greys and dark blues and bright waistcoats that he liked so much.

Thomas had summed up human nature very shrewdly. Harry Fallow was popular for his lively wit and hearty humour — his friends would have quickly lost patience with depression and low spirits, understandable though they might be.

The holiday over, Thomas went away to school and it was a doleful little sister who watched until the car was out of sight and then shed tears in solitude over the toys he had bestowed on her in his lordly manner.

Harry had intended to take his son to Wychwood but business, urgent and pressing, demanded his presence in Paris. So Thomas, excited and a little fearful now that the great day had arrived, kissed Louise, shook hands with Nanny and Standish and Mrs. Drew in an excess of sophistication, and climbed into the car, feeling very young and timid. Sitting up very straight and dignified, he did not look back at the house as the car drove away — knowing that the threatened tears would overflow with that last glance . . .

Thomas knew very little about Wychwood except that the Dawlish boys would be there and would show him the ropes. Thomas had never liked the Dawlish boys, thinking them childish and uncouth. They were spoiled by their doting mother and ignored by an indifferent father. He hoped he would not need to rely on them for friendship.

He was looking forward to the study of mathematics and history and languages. But he shrank from the thought of games. He was a sensitive child and saw little point in a handful of boys chasing a ball or hitting a ball with a bat and haring between two sets of stumps. He hoped that he would have plenty of opportunity to indulge in his favourite occupation — and wondered if he would be taught to understand art at the school . . .

As Louise had anticipated, the days were different without Thomas. Nanny was sharp and often irritable. She worried about the boy. Whenever Louise toyed with her food, lacking appetite, Nanny reminded her sharply that she doubted if her brother was enjoying such good food. On a wet, cold day when Louise was kept indoors, Nanny remarked dolefully that she expected her brother was sent out in all weathers and with no one to remind him to change his socks and shoes when he went in.

These and like remarks filled Louise with dread. Supposing something happened to Thomas and he never came home again? After all, Mummy had gone away one night and not come back. She had only been told that Mummy was dead and her conception of death was extremely vague. She merely knew that Mummy no longer came to kiss her goodnight, smelling of perfume and rustling in silks and taffetas and laughingly rubbing her furs against Louise's cheek. Never again had she come to the nursery to play with them, to ask them what they had been doing, to exclaim over their prowess in reading and writing or to be persuaded to join them for nursery tea.

Daddy was different, too. He did not come rushing into the nursery in high humour and call her his poppet and throw her high into the air, bestowing a toy or a bag of sweets or a new picture book on them all, his loud laugh ringing to the attics. He was sad and quiet, he seldom brought presents and he often drew her to him and kissed her gently . . . his eyes so sad that she wished that Mummy hadn't gone away and made everybody unhappy.

She was lonely without Thomas. At nights, tucked up in bed, tears came to dampen her pillow and her heart was empty and forlorn. She wanted Thomas to come home: she wanted

Mummy to come and kiss her and let her stroke her furs or finger the silken material of her dress; she wanted Daddy to be laughing and happy again.

Nanny was kind but always busy, always telling her to be good and play with her doll or look at a book, always preoccupied with the many demands made on her by the two babies, for Ann was little more yet.

Ann was too young to be interesting and too old to fascinate her as Sally did. She wanted to play with Louise's toys and hugged them to her breast, screaming fury if Louise tried to retrieve her possessions.

Sally lived in a world of her own, her tiny hands impotently grasping at air, smiles and chuckles and coos her only expressions of happiness, tears and screams her only outlet for frustration. Louise loved her but wished Nanny would allow her to hold her sometimes. Sometimes — and these were wonderful moments — she was allowed to brush the fine fair hair or touch the tiny fingers or kiss the smooth, satiny cheek. Louise helped Nanny with the ceremony of the bath, passing warm towels and soap and cotton wool and napkins — always asking questions and always being diverted from such interesting subjects as why Sally was so little, why she couldn't do anything for herself, why Mummy had died and where had Sally come from? Sally was more interesting than the lifeless Amanda, her bright hair curling about her fingers, the bright blue eyes gazing unblinkingly at Louise, seemingly innocent and wise at the same time. Louise wished that she had yellow hair. She and Ann were alike with the dark hair they had inherited from Daddy and the eyes that were neither blue nor grey.

Louise had little time for the fifteen-month-old Ann. She had spent too much time with Thomas and allowed his precocious influence to shape her thoughts and feelings. Ann was placid and even-tempered — except for the fits of wild fury which were more devastating because of their rarity and in this she resembled her father. She never cried even when she fell and hurt herself — and because she was at the toddling stage, she frequently tumbled. She would laugh heartily and then struggle to her feet and repeat the performance until she was distracted by something that Louise had and which she wanted. A singleminded and purposeful child, nothing would divert her until she had achieved the object she desired.

The weeks passed quickly for Louise, nevertheless. Her life was bound up with Nanny and her sisters; the nursery and the morning hours at the small private school across the square; dolls and toys and books. On fine afternoons, she went into the Square gardens with Nanny who pushed Sally in her pram and kept a firm hand on Ann's reins. Nanny would join a crony on a wooden seat and hand Ann over to Louise with the stern injunction to look after her and play happily together. Sally slept peacefully while Nanny gossiped and Louise obediently toted Ann about on the grass, envious of other little girls who seemed to be having such wonderful times with their games and shrieks and laughter . . .

And as the weeks passed, so Harry Fallow became reconciled to the loss of his wife. A man could not mourn for ever, he told himself confidently — not even for a wonderful woman like Sarah. She would have hated to see him miserable and dejected. She would understand his frequent evenings at the Club, the card games, the billiard sessions, the drinking bouts with his friends, the theatre visits and the parties.

He even began to cast his eye on an attractive figure, a shapely pair of legs, a neat ankle — and knew that his blood stirred when he met a pair of laughing eyes or recognized the provocation in the smile of a woman. He was a lusty man and it was difficult to remember that he was in mourning. He argued with himself; had Sarah ever been angry because of his roving eye? It had been a joke between them. What of the time when he had flirted outrageously with Nancy Richards? Sarah had laughed and mocked his poor taste: reviewing Nancy on their next meeting, he had decided that Sarah was right . . . that Nancy was not worth his attentions. What of the time when Sarah caught him kissing the new maid in his study . . . she had laughed but sent the girl packing and, remembering her as a provocative and saucy wench, he had not blamed Sarah.

She had been an understanding and loving wife: a really wonderful woman. He had loved her dearly but the past was behind him — and she would not expect him to be a celibate for the rest of his life.

At the theatre one evening, he smiled and nodded to Lord Stokes in his box, who was accompanied by his granddaughter, Melissa, a raven-haired girl with innocent blue eyes — a beauty with a temperament that matched her looks. Harry was reminded of her coming-out ball when Sarah had tapped his arm and said lightly: "That's a delightful girl, Harry. If you ever tire of me and want a divorce I shall recommend you to marry Melissa Stokes. She's worthy of you. Remember that your taste is atrocious and be advised by me."

He had laughed and retorted: "My taste can't be so bad, darling! I married you, remember — the loveliest woman in the world. Don't imagine I shall ever want to be rid of you, my sweet — you've got me for the rest of your life!"

He had not forgotten her light remarks. Melissa was very popular and much admired — and he idly wondered if she had married. If not, why not? She was twenty-two and sought after, not only for her fortune and social standing, but also for her beauty, intelligence and charm. He knew the rumours which had it that she had refused six proposals. Was she so selective? Or was it simply a case of knowing the one man to arouse her emotions?

Since that evening, he had thought of Melissa often. Perhaps it was early days to be thinking of another woman — but he could not forget that lovely face, that air of self-possession, that bewitching smile . . .

Louise finally received the promised letter from Thomas. It was months since he had been home. He had spent a holiday with a schoolfriend and Louise had been hurt by his reluctance to return to his own home after the first term at Wychwood. She had asked him to write to her and he had said airily that it would be bad enough having to write a weekly letter to their father. Then, at sight of her crestfallen face, he had relented and promised to write to her one day.

For some weeks, Louise had persistently asked Standish if a letter had come for her. Kindly but firmly he had denied it — and eventually she had ceased to put the daily enquiry.

But at last Ada came to the nursery with an envelope in her hand and a ready smile for Louise. She was in the secret and she knew that the letter had become the focal point of the child's narrow little world.

Louise was thankful that Ada had brought the letter. She liked the elderly maid who was always kind, always willing to talk about her sister's children, always pleased to spare the time to explain anything that troubled Louise. Half the pleasure of her letter would have vanished if Nanny had given it to her and demanded to know what Thomas had written. Or if Standish had brought it for he was a much feared and awe-inspiring personage.

So she took her letter and, with a little of her brother's arrogance, bade Ada lower her cheek for a kiss. With a smile, the woman bent to her height and graciously received the accolade.

Louise crept into the window seat and studied the envelope with its seal on the back. Daddy had given Thomas a set of notepaper and envelopes for his birthday, engraved with the family crest, and jokingly suggested that it might encourage him to write more often.

For a long time, she could not bring herself to open the envelope. It seemed a pity to break the lovely seal. At last her eagerness won the day . . .

Dear Louise,

I like this place very much and the other fellows are jolly decent and I've made lots of friends. We have plenty of lessons which I like and too many games which I don't like — but one has to take the rough with the smooth as Cripps Major says. He's my special friend and I had a jolly super time at his place in Kent last hols. I'm going to be an artist. We've got a new art master and he's jolly good and he says I have a decided gift. I mean to paint your picture first of all and make you as famous as me. Look after Ann and Sally and give them each a hug for me. I miss you loads.

Your loving brother,
Thomas Fallow.

Thus Thomas wrote — and tears stung her eyelids and crept stealthily down her rosy, rounded cheeks. It was the first letter she had ever received and she thought it was a wonderful letter.

Her tears flowed even more freely because at the end of his letter he had drawn in pencil a little girl with curly hair and a big smile and printed beneath it the words: *Portrait of Louise Fallow*.

A sob escaped her.

Nanny, having just entered the room, glanced at her suspiciously. "Are you crying, Louise?"

She shook her head. "Oh no, Nanny!"

41

"Hm! I hope you haven't caught cold . . . sniffing like that!" She turned to take some tiny garments from a drawer and Louise hastily secreted the letter in the pocket of her cardigan and brushed a hand quickly across her eyes. She knelt on the window-seat and looked down at the busy square. She recognized her father's car and watched as he stepped on to the pavement and then turned to give his hand to a very pretty lady. Daddy said something to her which caused her to smile. Then he looked up at the window and bent to speak to his companion with a nod towards the upper part of the house. Louise drew back quickly as the lady glanced up, suddenly shy. She wondered who the lady could be . . .

Some minutes later, Ada came to tell Nanny to brush Louise's hair and send her down to the drawing-room. Nanny raised her eyebrows. "Company?"

Ada nodded. "Feminine company at that — and very nice too," she said with excitement in her voice.

"That'll do, Ada!" Nanny sent a warning glance at Louise and then drew the child towards her and began her administrations.

Her little face soon glowed from a quick scrubbing with the flannel and her dark hair gleamed and was neatly smoothed to her head by the energetic brushing. She bore with it all patiently knowing that it was useless to question Nanny about the summons . . .

Harry leaned back in his chair and smiled at Melissa. She was beautiful in her deep blue dress: her hair, dark as night, was piled high on her head apart from a few rebellious curls which strayed about her ears.

It was almost a year since Sarah's death and he felt that he had been patient enough. He had been courting Melissa discreetly for the past few months and he felt that she might not be averse to a proposal of marriage.

He had already approached her grandfather. Lord Stokes had been dubious . . . and perfectly frank. He had hoped for a better match for Melissa: Fallows were a good family but not a wealthy one; and he was not too happy that she should marry a widower with four small children. He reminded Harry that she had refused several offers of marriage — why was he so confident of success? He did not think that Melissa would take him but he would not stand in the way of her happiness if it was what she wanted.

Harry had thought of those things for himself. He knew that it was presumptuous of him to expect her to marry him. He realized that a girl of twenty-three would have to be very much in love to take a man of thirty-eight, a widower with four children and very little income. He did not know if she loved him. He thought she was probably quite fond of him — and he hoped that she would marry him.

She returned his smile, a little shyly. "How old is your little girl, Harry?" she asked.

"The one at the window is

six — Louise. Ann is nearly two and the baby, as you know, is a year old in November." He felt slightly uncomfortable as she met his eyes steadily and knew that she was fully aware of his reluctance to give his youngest child her name.

"They're certainly very young . . . poor little things. They must miss their mother, Harry."

"Oh, I don't know," he said awkwardly. "Nanny is very capable and very kind — and my . . . Sarah didn't really have much to do with them, you know. I suppose I was a possessive husband."

She smiled at that faintly apologetic remark. "I imagine you would be," she said teasingly.

"Do you like children?" he asked abruptly.

"Yes, of course," she returned in some surprise. A trace of mischief lurked in her blue eyes. "But you wouldn't be able to afford any more, surely, Harry? And I might have a dozen — I'm still very young."

He stared at her. "I don't understand . . . "

She rose and went over to him. She
took his face between her hands and
kissed him almost tenderly on the lips.
"Could I make you happy, darling?"
she asked quietly.

He caught her hands and held them
firmly. "In every way," he said, almost
passionately.

"Then why haven't you asked me to
marry you?" she teased him indulgently.
"I know it's in your mind — and it isn't
leap year, you know. I don't want to be
forced to propose to you."

He rose and drew her into his arms.
"Do you mean it, Melissa? Would you
marry me?"

"Of course I would — gladly. I've
always loved you . . . ever since I
first saw you at my coming-out ball.
Didn't you know? I was madly jealous
of Sarah. I've never been able to think
of marrying any other man . . . oh,
Harry, I'm a horrible little beast! I

was sorry when Sarah died, naturally — but I couldn't help thinking that it might be the gateway to my happiness with you. I didn't really dare to hope that you'd even notice me . . . "

He stilled the words with his lips and she clung to him, carried away on a tide of love and longing. She did not know of the shadow that touched his eyes, the ache in his heart as he thought of the woman he had loved and would love until the end of time. He had a great affection for Melissa but she could never take Sarah's place in his heart. He could not live alone. A man needed a wife — and Melissa was all that he could desire . . . beautiful, intelligent, accomplished. She loved him and, by her own admission, she was devoted to children . . .

There was a timid tap at the door and he released her, forcing a smile to his stiff lips. "That must be Louise."

A little hesitant, Louise entered the room and met the blue, friendly eyes of the unknown visitor. She was encouraged by their warmth to approach her father who put out his hand and drew her towards him. With a swift smile for Melissa, he said quietly: "Louise, shake hands with Miss Stokes. She is going to be your new Mummy."

Louise stared without comprehension but obediently extended her hand. Melissa took it between both of her own hands and smiled down at her gently. "Let me kiss you," she said affectionately. "You're going to be my little girl, aren't you?" She held the child close and met Harry's eyes above the dark head. "She is like you, Harry."

He nodded. "The boy is the image of his mother. He's doing well at Wychwood, apparently — and you won't have to cope with him."

Louise looked up at the lady's lovely face. Then she said doubtfully: "My Mummy is dead and gone away."

"Yes, I know," Melissa assured her warmly. "So I'm going to live here and look after you as she would have done.

Your daddy is lonely and he needs someone to look after him, too."

Louise wrenched herself away and ran to her father. She tugged urgently at his sleeve. He looked down at her with a smile in his eyes and an amused quirk about his lips.

"Will you laugh and sing again, Daddy? Will you bring me presents?"

He touched her cheek with his hand in a careless gesture of affection. "I expect so, my poppet."

Melissa sighed. Harry looked up with a question in his eyes. She said softly: "How miserable you must have been, darling — if a child of that age noticed the change in you."

He brushed aside her words. "It's over and done with now, Melissa. Now we have the future before us — and I know we're going to be happy. You'll make me a wonderful wife — and my children will have a mother once more."

"May I see the others?" she asked, shyly.

He hesitated briefly. Then he nodded. "If you wish, darling. Louise, run up and ask Nanny to bring Ann and Sally to meet Miss Stokes. You can come down with her if you like."

As Louise went from the room, Harry crossed to the decanters to pour himself a drink. Melissa looked at him, a faint smile touching her lips. She recognized that he was apprehensive and still faintly bewildered by her willingness to marry him.

"She's a dear little girl," she said easily. "It's rather nice to be provided with a ready-made family, Harry."

He turned to look at her anxiously. "You're sure it won't be too much for you, Melissa. Four children — well, they can be quite a handful, you know."

"Surely not," she protested. "Anyway, I won't have to cope with them entirely on my own."

When Nanny came into the room, Melissa hurried to catch Ann into her arms and give her an impulsive hug,

50

undisturbed by the enigmatic stare and instinctive withdrawal of the child. "Oh, what a darling . . . she's sweet, Harry!" Ann wriggled in her arms, liking few people and always wary of strangers. With a little laugh that succesfully hid her chagrin for children usually went willingly to her side, Melissa set her down and turned to exclaim over the infant Sally with her yellow hair and big blue eyes. She took the baby into her arms and held her close, resting her cheek against the soft, silken mass of her hair.

Harry turned away on the pretext of refilling his glass. Melissa glanced at him and then abruptly thrust the baby back into Nanny's welcoming arms. The two women exchanged speaking glances of mutual understanding . . . and then Nanny went from the room, taking the two young children with her but leaving Louise to sit on the carpet and play with the gold locket that Melissa had taken from about her throat and given to her to examine.

Melissa went to Harry and linked her hand in his arm. "We'll be married soon, won't we, darling?" she said confidently.

He looked down at that youthful, lovely face — and swiftly banished the memory of Sarah. "Very soon," he assured her and kissed her cheek . . .

They were married two weeks later at a quiet, family ceremony — and if Harry doubted that he could give this lovely girl all the happiness and affection that she merited and if Melissa wondered if she could successfully erase all memory of her predecessor from his heart and mind, no one could have known as Harry almost overflowed with pride in his beautiful bride and her radiant happiness and unmistakable love quietened the doubts in the minds of her family and friends.

Harry carried his bride off to the Continent for an extended honeymoon tour. They planned to return on Christmas Eve, bringing with them trunkloads of presents for the children . . .

Thomas came home for the Christmas holidays. He did not indicate whether he approved or disapproved of his father's remarriage. He knew well that he would be rebuked if he dared to pass any opinion. The year at Wychwood had given him added maturity and he had learned to hide his sensitive nature beneath a veneer of boyish bravado which clashed badly with the occasional precocity of his manner.

He found Louise to be a sober little girl, quieter than was natural for her age. Her loneliness and lack of suitable friends had turned her thoughts inwards and she was no longer laughing and gay and full of idle chatter. Even the new mother and the promise of presents from abroad failed to stir her to excited anticipation. Thomas felt a momentary concern but his thoughts were too filled with his new way of life, his many friends and his future career as an artist. His talent had been recognized and encouraged by a percipient master and Thomas did not doubt that he would know the accolades of fame and success in time to come.

He was bored with the domestic blanket which fell on him as soon as he set foot inside the house. Nanny fussed him to the point of irritation. Louise clung so much that he felt oppressed by the weight of her affection and dependence. He did not like the undercurrents in the atmosphere and he was quick to realize that the servants did not welcome a new mistress and thought that his father had found consolation too soon.

He was even more arrogant since he had been at Wychwood: he was surprisingly intelligent and oddly unconcerned with the opinions of anyone but himself. He had executed a number of skilful water colours during the past term and he planned to offer them as a wedding present for his father and stepmother. He had persuaded Kennet to allow him to try his hand at a portrait in oils and it was amazingly clever — a good reproduction of his small sister — and he intended it to be her Christmas present.

The house was lavishly decorated with mistletoe, holly and paper bunting. A large laurel wreath hung on the front door with its bright red ribbon . . . but on Boxing Day it was replaced with another of waxen lilies and black ribbon. The house was swiftly stripped of festivity and once again plunged into mourning . . .

For Christmas morning brought the news that Harry and Melissa had been killed in a road accident on their way from Paris to Versailles.

Condolences and flowers streamed in. Harry had been a man of many friends, liked and respected in his social and business life. Melissa had been beautiful and popular — and the tragedy of her death at such an early age and while she was on her honeymoon touched the hearts of many.

Robert Fallow, Harry's brother,

hurried to make the necessary arrangements for the funeral — and then he was faced with the problem of Harry's children.

He was a good, kindly man. Like Harry in build and colouring, he lacked his brother's genial, careless heartiness but he earned liking and respect and friendship with his quiet, sympathetic and understanding manner. He was prepared to do his best for Harry's children. He had one child of his own, an adopted son named Martin, a few years older than Thomas. His wife had assured him that she would willingly take one of Harry's girls and bring her up as her own. She was a delicate, frail woman and although Robert would have opened his doors to all four of the children, he felt it would scarcely be a fair burden for Elizabeth's shoulders.

He had been fond of Harry and this double tragedy in thirteen months seemed a terrible thing. Certainly, his wife had shed many tears over the news — and it had not been easy for him to control his emotions.

Realizing the odd maturity in the boy, he talked to Thomas frankly, explaining that when he was twenty-one, the house would be his together with the majority of his father's income. The three girls would share the remainder as it was pretty likely that they would marry in due course.

Thomas listened courteously. He did not know whether or not to be pleased about the money. It would save him from artistic penury for he well knew that artists, like all creators, were invariably condemned to starve to death and were only acclaimed after their untimely demise. But he had a vague idea that one did good work only when moved by the pangs of hunger and the necessity to pay the rent — and he hoped the money would not prevent him from attaining the success which he hoped to enjoy in his lifetime!

"I suppose it's early days to ask you what you want to do with your future?"

Robert Fallow said tentatively.

"I know what I want, sir. I want to be an artist." The answer came confidently and without hesitation.

Robert looked at him with a faint smile. "I see. You've already made up your mind. You like painting, do you?"

"What do they say about your work at Wychwood? I didn't think they encouraged that kind of thing very much."

"They don't really . . . but Kennet . . . he's our art master and a jolly fine chap . . . he thinks I should make a name for myself one day."

"Well, we'll hope so, Thomas. I'm glad to hear that you have an aim in life, anyway. It's an excellent thing. I don't like drifters. So you want to study art seriously, do you?"

Thomas nodded. "Definitely, sir."

"That will mean the Slade when you've finished your schooling . . . well, time enough to arrange that, Thomas. But I won't forget what you've told me . . . "

He was several weeks at the house, trying to solve the problem of the three girls. He need not worry about Thomas: he was at an excellent school where he could stay until he was seventeen or eighteen. Then he could go to the Slade. He had definite ideas on what he wanted to do with his life, anyway. Art was a tricky kind of career but there was enough money to ensure that the boy did not starve until he tired of the life and made up his mind to abandon it for a more reliable career.

The infant Sally had captured his heart with her golden hair and bright blue eyes: he felt that Elizabeth would welcome the child and that she was young enough to be brought up as their own daughter. But there still remained the question of the other two girls . . . Louise was an odd child, introspective, almost sullen and he rarely knew how to deal with her . . . and Ann always made him feel ill at ease with her penetrating gaze and abrupt indifference.

He was relieved when a visitor was announced one day and he turned to greet Sarah's sister. Perhaps her visit meant the end of his dilemma . . .

Robert was struggling with a list of figures which represented Harry's business and personal incomes but as the door opened and Standish said, with that annoying hint of snobbery in his voice: "Lady St. Clair, sir," he rose to his feet and greeted her warmly. They had met once, many years ago . . . when Harry was married to Sarah. Now he smiled at an attractive woman in her middle thirties, well-dressed, slim and elegant and extremely self-possessed. He recalled that Bernice had married a wealthy baronet and was still without an heir although it was at least eight years since the wedding. Her husband was elderly and Robert wondered fleetingly if the fault lay at St. Clair's door.

"What a terrible thing!" she exclaimed without preamble. "I've been in

Norfolk . . . staying with friends. I've only just heard the news. Poor Harry! I suppose he'd had his share of happiness and unkind Fate decided not to allow him any more. On his honeymoon . . . a terrible thing! And that beautiful, sweet girl . . . oh, I shall miss Melissa very much!"

"Do sit down," Robert invited. "May I offer you coffee?"

"Thank you. You're Robert Fallow . . . I met you at the wedding — it seems a lifetime ago!"

"Twelve years," he reminded her delicately.

"It must be! Well, what is happening to the children?" She came directly to the point and he remembered that she had always been noted for her bluntness. Far from being offended, he appreciated it at such a time. She recognized, where so many others would fail to do so, that the children were an important matter to be solved as soon as possible. "How old is the boy? Eleven, I suppose?"

"Yes. He's at Wychwood, you know. An excellent school and I think you will agree that he can come to no harm if he stays there."

"There's enough money to pay for his education?"

"Yes. Harry enjoyed a substantial income." He added discreetly: "Melissa had quite an income of her own, too — a most attractive dowry for any bride."

"Francis Stokes is very cut up about this awful business," she said bluntly. "Hard on him . . . very! The girl's mother ran off with an Italian, you know — and died of some disease in Italy. Charles Stokes shot himself . . . The old man doted on Melissa — she was all he had. Now he only has his memories." She sighed briefly. Then she collected her wandering thoughts and said firmly: "Well, Thomas seems to be settled. He'd better come to us during the school holidays unless he has other plans." She glanced at Robert. "My husband and I are prepared to take one of the girls. You'll understand that while Thomas is always welcome to stay at Merion Hall, it wouldn't be fair to adopt him." She paused delicately. "I'm still reasonably young and we are hoping for an heir one day. Naturally, if I had a son, he would naturally take precedence in the matter of estate and title over an adopted child. If I don't give George a son . . . well, the estate and title will revert to his eldest nephew . . . and that would be rather hard on Thomas if he'd been brought up to expect some kind of inheritance."

"I do understand, of course," Robert assured her. "Er . . . my wife and I are offering a home to the youngest child."

Bernice nodded, silent for a brief moment. "That unfortunate child," she said. "Good of you to take a child of such tender age."

He leaned forward. "I'm going to ask a kindness of you, Lady St. Clair. You say that you're willing to adopt one of the girls. Louise is six years old: Ann is two. They are alike in colouring and looks. My wife is delicate and I feel that one child is all that she could cope with . . . particularly as Sarah is still a baby. I have no other relatives who might give a helping hand — and you are Sarah's only sister. Your brother, I believe, is a bachelor and lives abroad." He paused and cleared his throat.

Before he could continue, she said with a smile: "If I adopt Louise you will find it difficult to provide for Ann — or vice versa. So you want me to take them both."

She regarded him steadily and with a hint of amusement in the curve of her mouth.

He spread his hands wide. "It's a difficult position . . . "

"Yes, I agree. Oh, I've no objection. It's a pity to separate the children but necessity drives us. I'll take Louise and Ann."

"Your husband . . . " He paused with a query in the lift of his eyebrow.

She smiled as Standish came into the room with the coffee tray. "George gets on very well with children. And I believe he thinks that by adopting one of Sarah's girls I might at last provide him with an heir." She glanced at him obliquely through long lashes and he was reminded forcibly that she was a lovely woman. "It can happen," she added, almost to herself.

Robert thought to himself that Bernice St. Clair was not a happy woman. Possibly her lack of a child weighed heavily on her heart. He was glad that she had so quickly taken up his hint and he was relieved that the futures of the children were ascertained at last. He felt instinctively that Bernice would do her best for the girls: they would have a fine home and a good upbringing: St. Clair was a wealthy man and they might benefit more from a life at Merion Hall than if Harry had lived. Bernice was a fair-minded woman: he felt she would be kind and affectionate and the kinship was close enough for her to feel sincere concern for the girls.

He watched her deft movements with the heavy silver pot and unconsciously admired her innate grace and her ease of manner. They drifted into general conversation as they sat over the coffee and cigarettes . . .

Louise was bewildered by the sudden turn of events. One day she had an adoring Daddy and a new Mummy: the next day she was told in muted accents that they would not be coming home. She had been enveloped in Nanny's huge embrace and wriggled with embarrassment as tears were shed above her head. She did not need to be told that her father was dead and to her childish mind it seemed that people made a habit of going away for ever . . . the people she loved and needed.

Thomas explained very simply that they would not live in the big house where they had been born in the future. He was going back to school: Uncle Robert was taking Sally to his house and she and Ann would live with Aunt Bernice who was very nice and would be kind to them.

Her lips quivered. "Won't *you* ever be coming back?"

She had not understood and he felt a momentary impatience. Then he reminded himself that she was, after all, five years his junior. "One day when I'm a man," he assured her. "Then the house will be mine. Until then you must stay with Aunt Bernice and be a good girl. But when we're all grown up we shall live here together just like now."

"Is Nanny going to stay here till then?"

He shook his head. "Nanny is going to live with some other children. Aunt Bernice thinks that you are old enough to have a governess . . . but I expect she has a Nanny to look after Ann."

She wrinkled her forehead. "What's a guvness?"

"A very nice lady who will teach you to sew and play the piano and

67

draw nicely. She'll show you how to do sums and how to find England on a map and tell you all about the kings and queens of England. You'll find it jolly interesting." Thomas knew all about governesses from his holiday visits to the Kentish home of Cripps Major. He did not add that his friend's sisters plagued their governess with the various tricks and jokes that they learned from Cripps Major.

"I like Uncle Robert," she announced unexpectedly and he realized that she had not been listening to his glowing recital.

He said with faint impatience: "Well, you can't live with *him*. You're going to live with Aunt Bernice and Uncle George."

"Why am I?"

"Because it's all been arranged," he muttered.

"Where are you going to live?"

"I shall be at school, silly — but I expect I'll come to stay with Aunt Bernice occasionally during the hols.

It won't really be so different, Lulu," he added swiftly as the tears began to trickle down her cheeks.

"Why can't we all live together?" she wailed.

He dried her cheeks with his own grubby handkerchief. "Because Uncle Robert hasn't room for all of us — and Aunt Bernice hasn't got any little girls and she wants you and Ann to live with her. Don't cry . . . you've got to be brave and look after Ann."

Although he comforted her, he knew that their lives would never be the same again. He did not mind so much because he accepted the fact of growing up and the inevitable change — and also because very little really mattered to him but his determination to be an artist.

He went back to Wychwood within a few days. He did not mind the badge of orphan for it was likely to bring him a brief popularity among his fellows and certainly the masters would not expect him to apply too diligently to his studies while he carried the burden of grief . . .

Bernice St. Clair returned to her husband and home the following day — and Louise and Ann accompanied her. Nanny wept copiously at the parting and her tears were infectious. Bernice swept two pathetic bundles of misery into the car with an exasperated glance at Nanny, almost regretting her impulsive generosity towards her nieces. But during the drive into Surrey, she managed to divert the girls with toys and picture-books and richly-embroidered stories of their new life. She found that Ann was easily diverted but Louise clung to Amanda and stared through the car window with tears glistening in her eyes for a long time before she was finally tempted by the blandishments which her aunt offered.

Robert Fallow stayed only to dismiss the servants and close up the house. Standish and his wife, who was cook, offered to remain as caretakers and because they were a little old to seek new positions, Robert agreed, certain that they could be trusted to keep the house in good repair and good order.

He had found a young, capable girl to act as a nurse for Sally, feeling that Nanny had long outlived her usefulness. He imagined that her ideas were old-fashioned and it was much better for the child to have the care of a young, pretty and sweet-smelling girl of eighteen. He was glad of her presence during the journey into Kent for Sally cried heartily and long as though she sensed the separation from her family and familiar surroundings — and Robert knew that he would have been incapable of stemming her sobs and tears.

Elizabeth came to the door of the pleasant, rambling house at the sound of the car, eager to embrace the niece they were adopting, her motherly arms aching to hold a baby once more. Her own children had died within a few days of birth and when she was advised to have no more, they had adopted Martin.

Robert took Sally from the nurse and turned to his wife. "Well, my dear — here's your new daughter, safe and sound and slightly damp!"

"She's a lovely little girl!" Elizabeth exclaimed, taking her from him and holding her close. "I must take her to show Martin!"

Robert smiled indulgently. "Nonsense, my dear! Martin's too old to care for babies. But take the child into the house, by all means."

Martin Fallow was in the library, his dark head bent over a book. He was a tall lad of sixteen, thin and sensitive and attractive in an austere way. His parents were a little shy of this studious, somewhat aloof boy they loved as dearly as if he were their own son.

Elizabeth called excitedly: "Look, Martin!"

He glanced up. Sally smiled broadly and he was instantly captivated by that lovely, innocent, friendly smile. Throwing aside his book, he leaped to his feet and moved to his mother's side. He touched Sally's small, soft hand and knew a swift enchantment as her fingers curved about his own. "Why, she's lovely," he said slowly. "A golden girl."

Sally gurgled with merriment. A tenderness touched the boy's lips and eyes.

"It will be so difficult not to spoil her," Elizabeth sighed. "I fell in love with her on sight — she's so sweet, isn't she? That lovely hair and those big blue eyes." She hugged the child and kissed her impulsively. "My little Sally," she said warmly.

Martin frowned. "No, Mother . . . not Sally. It's a pity to spoil her name. I shall call her Sarah."

2

THE Autumn Exhibition opened at Schnell's Bond Street gallery at the end of September. The next day, a new artist was acclaimed by the critics and their praise was repeated throughout social circles.

Eventually, it reached the ears of Robert Fallow, sitting over a glass of brandy and an aromatic cigar in the quiet peace of his club. He pricked up his ears at the name and an acquaintance leaned forward to say loudly: "Any relative of yours, Fallow . . . this young artist chap they're all talking about?"

Robert smiled. "My nephew — brother Harry's boy. You remember Harry? Killed in a car crash nine years ago?"

"Lord, yes! This is his son, eh? Doing well for himself." The man chuckled. "Merely proves that parents aren't always necessary, eh . . . I sometimes think we get on better without them." He snapped his fingers at a waiter. "Let me buy you a drink, Fallow . . . what shall it be? Brandy?"

For an hour or so he sat with the military man while they discussed not only Harry and his young bride, Thomas Fallow's prospects and triumphs . . . *'made, my dear chap, absolutely made now that Lady Crombie is taking an interest!'* . . . but also current affairs, politics and the likelihood of a general election that year and the sad decline in the type of member that was to be found in the club of latter years.

At last, Robert managed to escape and as he drove home to The Meads, he was at liberty to think of young Thomas. He was just twenty, amazingly young for his work to have impressed the critics so forcibly, and it seemed that he had chosen a career that held much promise. Leaving school at seventeen, he had turned down the suggestion of university and also vetoed Robert's mention of the Slade School of Art. He had chosen to go to Paris to live on the Left Bank among people of his own kind, learning art the hard way. A year later, he had gone to Italy and studied art under one of the great masters. Schnell had been persuaded to take an interest in his work — and thus the exhibition which displayed several of his paintings.

Thinking of Thomas naturally led him to thoughts of Sarah. She was ten years old now and very intelligent. For some time, he had been debating the wisdom of telling her that she was an adopted child and that she had a brother and two sisters. She frequently plied them with questions which were sometimes difficult to answer and required evasive replies. Now she was old enough to understand — and he decided impulsively to take Sarah to Schnell's Gallery to see her brother's talented work and meet Thomas in person. He felt that she should not be denied contact with her family. She would be thrilled to meet her brother — and the girls who had known such a happy home with Bernice and George. Despite the lack of an heir, they were treated as their own children and very much loved. Once or twice, Bernice had brought them to The Meads but Sarah had always been told that they were her cousins.

Arriving home, he found Sarah waiting on the perch. "You're late, Daddy," she accused as he approached.

He kissed her fair cheek. "I've been with a friend at the club, my child. Where is your mother?"

"She's gone to her room . . . she isn't very well. Miss Lake told me to go to bed but I slipped out to wait for you."

"That was naughty of you," he said but the reproof lacked conviction. "It's getting cold — and Miss Lake will blame me if you catch a chill."

She wrinkled her nose mischievously. They went into the house and she poured his coffee and urged him into his favourite chair, noting the weariness about his eyes. Then she sat down on a low stool close to his chair and he laid a hand on her shoulder. She was very dear to him. Intelligent, calm and lovely, tall and slender; the slim bones of her face were beautifully classic and he knew that she would be a lovely woman. But her mother had been a beauty, too . . .

He loosened the mass of her golden hair from its restraining bands and it rippled past her shoulders to her waist. He twined his fingers in the molten gold strands, listening to her chatter, answering her questions. He knew that he should send her to bed but this was a very pleasant interlude . . . and he felt that the time was ripe to talk to her as an adult . . . to tell her the things she was old enough to know . . . yet the right opening eluded him for some time.

At last he said quietly: "Would you like to go to London with me next week, Sarah? A new artist is showing his work in a Bond Street gallery . . . I think you should see it. It's educational and interesting so I don't think we'll meet with opposition from Miss Lake. I want you to meet the artist, too."

She turned her eager face towards him. "I'd love that, Daddy." She was always delighted whenever he proposed an outing. "Who's the artist?"

"His name is Thomas Fallow."

She wrinkled her forehead. "Is he a relative, Daddy? I don't know anyone called Thomas."

He laughed, teasing her. "Come, Sarah . . . you've heard Louise mention him often enough."

Again that slight frown. Then she nodded. "Oh, that one! Louise says he's her brother . . . this mysterious Thomas. She told me that she and Ann are adopted . . . that they don't really belong to Aunt Bernice and that their name is Fallow, like ours. Is it true, Daddy?"

"You've never asked me about this before," he evaded.

She shrugged. The movement was inexpressibly graceful. "It wasn't important. But now that you've mentioned his name . . . is he Louise's brother?"

"It's a long story," he said slowly, reluctantly. "You'd better go to bed, Sarah — and I'll tell you another time."

The familiar hint of obstinacy touched her eyes. "Daddy!" she reproached. "You brought up the subject — and you must have had a reason. So now you must tell me the story . . . I'm really not tired. I'll get you some more coffee and you can light your pipe and be really comfortable."

He laughed — and obediently stretched out his hand to his pipe and pouch. Sarah poured fresh coffee into his cup. Then she turned an attentive face towards him, swinging her long hair impatiently from her shoulders.

"It's a long story," he warned again.

"Good . . . I love stories. Please, Daddy — don't tease!"

"You may not like this story," he said reluctantly. "It concerns you . . . I only hope I'm not making a mistake in thinking you old enough to hear it."

"Oh, of course not," she said impatiently. "Come on . . . you've roused my curiosity."

"Very well." He took a deep breath and began to tell her about her mother who had died at her birth, her father's re-marriage a year later and his tragic death on his honeymoon, of Bernice St. Clair's impulsive generosity in taking Louise and Ann into her home and of his own desire for a daughter and the decision to adopt Sarah, of Thomas and his years at Wychwood before going to Paris and then to Rome and his long ambition to be an artist . . .

Sarah cradled her chin in her hands and listened intently. He could not guess at her reactions or her thoughts. When he had finished, she said slowly: "So you are really my uncle? And Martin . . . he isn't my brother at all?"

"No, no. Martin is my son — and your cousin."

She nodded thoughtfully. "What was my father's name?"

"Henry . . . but he was always called Harry."

"What was he like?"

"Oh, gay and merry and well-liked. Full of fun — tall and dark . . . we resembled each other," he said diffidently.

"And Louise and Ann are really my sisters? But they're not a bit like me, Daddy."

"No . . . you're the image of your mother, Sarah. And you were given her name."

She scanned his face. "So Louise was telling the truth. Thomas is her brother — and mine, too. Why did she know — and why haven't I ever met him?"

"Louise remembers him, I expect. She was six when your father was killed . . . you were only a baby. You did meet Thomas once but you were too small to remember it. He was at Merion Hall when we stayed there one summer. You were only about three at the time. He's been abroad since he left school but now he's back in England and I've had a letter from him. He wants to meet you . . . he has never wanted to lose touch with his sisters. I believe he and Louise frequently exchange letters."

"Thank you for explaining everything," she said politely, so formally that he was hurt, feeling that she had withdrawn her affection from him abruptly. Then, impulsively, she scrambled on to his knee and threw her arms about his neck. "I love you just the same, Daddy. You're still my father . . . that other man doesn't mean anything at all!"

He kissed her smooth cheek. "But you want to meet your famous brother, don't you?"

"Is he famous?" She drew back sharply.

He pursed his lips. "Well, he soon will be — he's already making his name known. He's a clever young man and one day we'll all be proud of him." He stroked her long, bright hair. "Now, look at the time, darling — run along to bed like a good girl."

She climbed down and went to the door. Then she turned and said lightly: "I won't sleep — my head is too full of everything. I'll be too busy thinking of my sisters and my famous brother!"

He laughed. "Nonsense! You're half asleep now. Goodnight, darling."

Slowly, Sarah mounted the stairs. She knew that she would not sleep. Her brain was whirling . . . yet in her heart she was glad that she knew the truth. Often and often she had wondered at her bright golden hair when Daddy, Mummy and Martin were all so dark. Sometimes she had felt that she was an alien element in the house . . . a feeling which she had hastily dismissed because she was so much loved, her every wish so readily granted. A weaker character would have been ruined irreparably long before . . . but Sarah Fallow had an indomitable spirit and a strong will . . .

She had always liked Louise St. Clair, always known a vague feeling of affinity with the older girl — but she had not been able to analyse her emotions. They were feelings and nothing more. She had sensed the staunch affection which Louise felt for her — and realized that she had always tried to mother and protect her.

Ann was different. She was a difficult girl to like . . . not in the least like Louise except in looks. She was a gay, laughing, careless girl who never took anything seriously and followed her own rules for living — defying convention at an early age. But Louise was quiet and serene, calm and reserved and very reassuring in her calmness. She was slim and dark-haired with blue-grey eyes and a piquant loveliness. She was accomplished, a credit to the teaching of her governess and the training of Bernice St. Clair. They had coped easily with Louise and found her a charming child but the madcap Ann was almost impossible to control.

Louise could play the piano with a neat and competent execution; she spoke fluent French and Italian with good accents; her water-colour sketches were weak but charming; she plied her needle industriously and to good effect; she was well-mannered and obedient and eager to please.

Ann showed a brilliant execution on the piano when she chose . . . she had never needed tuition for she had an instinctive ear for music. When she did not choose, she was apt to thump out wild discords or strum violently from one note to another without connection. She hated languages and her accent and vocabulary were more than eccentric. She affected to despise art in all forms and certainly her daubs owed nothing to artistic talent. She would not sew unless compelled — and then the finished article was crumpled and soiled and inevitably bloody from pricked fingers. She adored riding and at every opportunity would mount her mare and gallop over the fields . . . she had sneered at the idea of a gentle pony when she was nine years old. She swam like a fish, climbed trees like a boy, explored the estate with the village children and gave not a fig for convention or social graces.

Sarah liked and admired Louise . . . but she was more than a little afraid of the tempestuous Ann who jeered her reluctance to ride the restless mare and accused her of being a namby-pamby because she liked to sit and nurse her dolls or read a book or talk quietly to Louise instead of careering madly about the gardens and woods with Ann who was only a year older and therefore expected to be her contemporary.

Sarah lay wakeful in the dark and her mind etched pictures on her closed lids. She tried to visualize her brother Thomas and failed. She wondered what it would be like to meet him — and with some trepidation thought of the coming ordeal for she was shy and sensitive to snubs, real or imagined. With the dawn, she finally slept . . . and the rising sun invaded her bedroom to touch her golden hair to an aureole of light and illumine her sweet and lovely face to an almost ethereal beauty.

She was lying on her face in the grass by the river a few days later. Her hair, loosed from its bands, flowed to her waist and was a molten mass of gold in the sunshine. She watched the minnows and softly sang to herself in a clear, musical tone. She heard a step, the crackle of a twig, and looked up. Then she was on her feet and running into the arms of the tall, sunburnt man who welcomed her with affection tinged with his natural reserve.

"Martin!" She hugged him violently. "When did you get home?"

"Half an hour ago," he said, gently disengaging himself from her embrace. "Well, my golden girl, you're looking well — have you been a good girl?"

He felt aeons older than this child from the superiority of his twenty-five years. What a beautiful child she was — his golden girl indeed! He smiled at the thought of the nickname he had bestowed on her. His appreciative eye ran over the classic lines of her face and slight body. Her hair gleamed like gold and shone from energetic brushing. She moved gracefully — and yet there was a hint of proud arrogance in every movement. Her voice was musical and well-modulated. He thought that she had matured a little during the past years. He had been in many countries and had seen many beautiful women of all nationalities and colours. Yet now, gazing down into this child's lovely face, he felt that it was much better to be home and greeted with the limpid adoration in Sarah's blue eyes, to know the eager embrace of her childish affection.

"Oh, of course." She dismissed his question. "But how tanned you are! I wish I'd been with you!" And she sighed a heartfelt sigh for the drawbacks of childhood.

He smiled. "One day we'll travel together, my Sarah," he promised. "I'll show you the world."

She sat on the grass and drew him down to her side. His hand rested lightly on hers for a moment then he gently stroked the mass of her hair. Her face was very serious. She toyed with a blade of grass and would not look at him as she said quietly: "Martin, did you know that I'm not your sister?"

He looked at her sharply. His father had warned him to guard his tongue, explaining that Sarah knew of her adoption and he was not sure that she was happy about it.

"Yes, I've always known. You're my cousin — but I've never thought of you as anything but a little sister." He smiled indulgently. "I remember the day Father brought you here," he said reminiscently. "Mother and I were so delighted with you . . . you were like a golden-haired doll with big blue eyes and a sweet smile."

"Do you know Thomas?" she demanded.

He looked his surprise. "Yes, I've met him," he admitted slowly.

"Then tell me all about him," she demanded eagerly. "Daddy isn't any good at description — and I don't like to ask Mummy. She's upset that I know the truth. She'd have liked me to believe I was her real daughter for the rest of my life. She possibly thinks I won't love her so much now. But that's ridiculous. Please tell me about Thomas."

A sudden thought struck him and he sought in his coat for his wallet. He riffled through its contents and drew out a sheet of drawing-paper, roughly torn from a block, and handed it to Sarah. "Thomas gave me this when we met in Rome. He says it's a self-portrait but I think he was joking. See what you make of it."

She studied the drawing. The few, flowing lines made no complete format yet she knew instantly what Thomas was like — a young man with a serious approach to life, a dedicated man, a sensitive, even sentimental man — and her heart leaped with pleasure. She could like this man! "May I keep this?" she asked quietly.

"Of course. But I can't make head or tail of it. It doesn't even look like a sketch."

"Oh, but it does!" she protested impulsively. "Look here . . . and here . . . " She pointed out the characteristics which were so clear to her eyes but Martin shook his head.

"No, I can't see it, child. But his work is all as abstract as that — and the critics rave about it so perhaps one needs a discerning eye. You seem to have it . . . I know I haven't. Thomas laughs at my taste but I like a portrait that conveys something!"

It was an excited child who accompanied Robert Fallow to Bond Street the following week. Martin had made his excuses and confided his aversion to modern art. Robert was no supporter of it yet he was eager to see Thomas' work for himself.

The gallery was crowded for all society flocked to the exhibition, partly to see the paintings which attracted so much notice and partly in the hope of seeing Thomas Fallow, who was reputedly young and handsome and charming.

Robert was acknowledged and greeted by several acquaintances and he paused to talk to an old friend who chucked Sarah beneath the chin and said that she was a lucky girl to claim relationship to the young artist. Sarah smiled absently and craned her neck around his bulk to look for Thomas.

At last, Robert realized her impatience and he stemmed his friend's garrulous flow and made his excuses. He smiled down at Sarah. "I'm sorry, child. Ah, there's Thomas!"

Her eyes flew towards the tall, slender man who was engaged in an argument with a bearded man. Her heart skipped a beat and then thudded heavily against her ribs. She could not mistake that crop of bright yellow hair, those intelligent blue eyes, the high intellectual brow and the warm, slightly sensual mouth.

Thomas glanced towards them carelessly — and then his eyes were touched with instant warmth and eagerness as he saw his uncle and the girl by his side. Breaking off his argument, he hurried to meet them, gazing at Sarah with affectionate admiration.

"Delightful!" he exclaimed. A smile hovered about his mouth. "I'm determined to paint you, Sally." He shook hands with his uncle. "Good afternoon, Uncle Bob. So you brought Sally with you?"

Sarah frowned. She had never been called Sally and she did not approve of the diminutive.

He touched her shoulder briefly. "Come and look at my feeble efforts, Sally," he invited. "Uncle Bob, I'm sure that modern art isn't to your taste. Please go into the office and join Schnell in a glass of sherry. He's expecting you and he has a really excellent sherry to offer you. I'll take care of Sally."

Robert accepted his dismissal gracefully, faintly amused. He had met and liked Schnell and was only too pleased to escape from the heat and the crush of the room.

Thomas smiled down at Sarah. "You will sit for me, won't you? Or would you rather see some of my work before you agree? You may not think that it's good enough."

She was tongue-tied, a rare state of affairs. But she was awed by his sophistication and worldliness, his god-like good looks, and shyness overwhelmed her. She was vaguely flattered by the manner which hinted that he thought of her as an adult with a mind of her own.

She walked down the length of the room by his side. She stopped in front of a canvas which to an unimaginative eye would have represented little but a medley of grey and white strokes. Sarah said immediately: "But that's Louise!"

Thomas was delighted and impressed. "You clever child!" he exclaimed. "You recognized her without difficulty." He smiled. "Do you know that Louise studied it for ten full minutes — and then asked me what it was supposed to represent! I suppose you can't tell me how you knew it was Louise?"

Sarah smiled, looking up at him triumphantly. "Of course I can! She is all greys and whites — quiet, colourless, calm and peaceful. If it was a picture of Ann, it would be all bright and glowing with bold, dashing strokes."

He caught her to him and gave her an affectionate hug. He could scarcely conceal his surprise and jubilation. "Brilliant! Sally, you're marvellous. Do you know how I'd portray you?" She shook her head. "All gold and pink and white," he declared, "rising out of a misty blue and green sea — and I'd call it 'Morning Sunrise'."

She released herself. She was still a little shy and his ardent enthusiasm was alien to her expectations. But she remembered her conviction of his dedication to art — and decided that his manner was merely its display.

She moved on to another canvas which she studied for some time. When she turned to him, she seemed bewildered. "Well?" he prompted anxiously.

"I know what it conveys — but I don't know who it is," she said slowly.

"Tell me what you see."

"A man with his head in his hands. There's sadness and despair and loneliness." She gave a little shiver. "I don't like it . . . it gives me a strange feeling."

Again he was startled by her discernment. Although the critics and the public professed to think his work little short of miraculous, he knew that the majority were compelled to refer to the catalogue before they could speak with any certainty on the subject of each painting. This one he had called 'Man With Bowed Head'. The sombre hues and stark lines should convey the remainder.

"Who is it?" Sarah asked.

He hesitated briefly. Then he said quietly: "My father, Sally . . . I saw him like that when my mother died. I was contemptuous then . . . I didn't understand." He gave a little laugh. "I tried to draw something like that on Louise's slate — and our Nanny was horrified."

Sarah said: "But he wasn't a bit like that! Daddy said that he was always laughing and gay and full of fun. I don't want to think of him like that."

He slipped his arm about her shoulders. "He wasn't unhappy for long," he said reassuringly. "He loved life too much. One day I'll do another portrait of him as he really was . . . you'll like that better."

She looked up at him. "Why do you call me Sally?"

He smiled. "Because you were always called Sally when you were a baby. But if you prefer Sarah, then I'll try to remember. You can see the other paintings another time. Let's join Schnell and Uncle Bob. I want to talk to you."

As they were about to leave the gallery, an hour later, Thomas exclaimed: "There's Louise with Aunt Bernice! How opportune! We must persuade them to have tea with us." He bounded across the road, ignoring the traffic.

A few minutes later, he returned, accompanied by his aunt and sister. Louise sent Sarah a slow, affectionate smile — and she was conscious of the familiar feeling of affinity.

"A family gathering," Thomas said happily.

"Thomas!" Louise remonstrated mildly as a passer-by turned to look at the jubilant young man. "Do you want the whole of Bond Street to hear you? You may be an artist but don't let us have displays of your

99

eccentricity in public." Her reproving words held a note of amusement and her smile banished the sting. She held out her hands to Sarah. She was a very self-possessed young woman, seemingly older and more sophisticated than her fifteen years. "How nice to see you, Sarah — and how pretty you look!" She smiled at her uncle and gave him her hand. "How are you, Uncle Robert?"

They exchanged pleasantries for a moment or two and then he turned to speak to Bernice St. Clair. She was still attractive but a little plump these days. "I hope you will have tea with us, Bernice?"

She chuckled. "Thomas has already swept Louise and Sarah halfway down Bond Street." She laid her fingers on Robert's arm and they followed the young people, talking amicably.

"He seems very impetuous. I've always thought of him as a very controlled young man," Robert said indulgently.

"His success is acting as an

intoxicant," Bernice said lightly.

Louise turned as they caught up with them. "Oh, don't you think it's wonderful, Uncle Robert? I've heard so many people talk of Thomas and his work and they say he's quite brilliant, a genius, a most talented artist."

Thomas and Sarah walked on, the former talking rapidly and excitedly to his little sister. Robert smiled down at Louise. "Don't believe all you hear, my dear," he warned gently. "People are only too ready to raise their voices in praise when more experienced connoisseurs of the arts lead the way. Your brother's work is different, novel. This success might not last and Thomas would be foolish to bank too much on it."

"Thomas is a little proud and arrogant," she admitted fairly. "But he's never been conceited without cause. That isn't one of his failings."

As they sat in the small restaurant over tea and pastries, Louise snatched an opportunity to turn to Sarah. "I expect you find Thomas a little bewildering," she said quietly. "But he's a very nice person, really — and usually very reserved and charming. Don't allow his high spirits to give you a wrong impression."

Thomas was inwardly amused by the number of people who flocked to give him commissions during the next few months. He knew that a few were shrewd and percipient, realizing that his work might be a little beyond average understanding but in time would probably be much in demand. Others came because Lady Crombie had been his first sitter and as the current leader of the society set she started a new fashion. Thomas Fallow became the vogue. He was extremely handsome, charming and intelligent: he had a way with women — and so it was that most of his sitters were lovely women who sought a new excitement.

They were not always pleased with the results and it was often embarrassing to have their friends demand an explanation of the 'monstrosity' which adorned their salons. But they hid their embarrassment with a supercilious air and replied: "My dear! Surely you must recognize Thomas Fallow's work? He's quite wonderful . . . Lady Crombie recommended him and I'm delighted with the result. He has such a wonderful appreciation of personality!" And, discomfited, the critics would take refuge in silence or a change of subject.

His amusement was tinged with contempt for the foolish who commissioned him while completely blind to the skilful artistry of his work, insensible to the delicate insight of nuances and shades of colour. He wished he could be honest enough to refuse such commissions but amusement overcame integrity and his fees were little short of exorbitant.

On one occasion, Louise remonstrated with him about the fee he demanded for a portrait of the Honourable Jessica Franklyn. He smiled and said lightly:

"I'm the new fashion, Louise dear — and all new fashions are highly expensive. If these people did not pay highly for my work they would consider it inferior. Besides, they like to boast of how much they paid — their friends are impressed and come to me for a similar service at similar cost."

His services were in great demand and he was always busy. It was his habit to pose the sitter and study him for an hour or more, his chin cupped in his hand or, hands in pockets, striding about his studio. He was considered eccentric but he needed to pierce the armour of worldly sophistication which so many of his sitters had erected about their true personalities and characters — and he knew that invariably they were disconcerted by his odd but penetrating gaze. Towards the end of an hour, they would either become restless or irritable or confused or remain patient — with a change of mood came through exactly what Thomas sought — the real person beneath the veneer. Then he would smile, apologize for his bad manners, offer them tea or a drink — and when they had gone, set to work like a man possessed with canvas and brushes, eager to capture the impression he had received before it faded. There were times when it was impossible to find what he sought — and then he would politely explain that the mood was lacking and request them to come another day.

Sometimes, concentrated study was unnecessary. A glance, a smile, the cadence of a voice, the rustle of skirts or a masculine gesture was sometimes enough and he would erect a canvas and work feverishly, talking to the sitter so that the glow of personality would not fade even as he worked.

Louise visited him at the studio several times a week. He had moved into the house on Cavendish Square, the house of his childhood, and converted the two attic rooms into a studio, having the slates of the roof removed and great panes of glass inserted to provide plenty of light.

He entertained lavishly, recognizing the importance of keeping in the public eye, of maintaining his foot inside the door of society. Soon, his soirées, his dinner parties, his musical evenings — and the unfailing gift he always pressed on each of his lady guests — were often the subject of comment — and always approving comment.

Thomas found his sister's company both pleasant and restful. He could work without interruption despite her presence and Louise did not besiege him with appeals for explanations. He knew that his work baffled her completely — and they both accepted it. He liked her to act as his hostess when he entertained for, although she was so young, she was perfectly at her ease and had been well trained in the social graces and conventions by Bernice St. Clair.

Bernice, at Louise's instigation,

frequently invited Sarah to stay with them at the London house and Robert could not find it in his heart to refuse the generous, kindly woman or the obvious eagerness of Sarah to accept the invitations.

Thomas found a sympathetic spark in his youngest sister. She had an unerring eye for his subject — providing she knew the sitter — and even at times advised him on minor points. He never resented her advice. He invariably found it to be good, sensible and reliable. It was sometimes difficult to remember that she was a mere child for she had a convincing maturity and the poise of a woman. She had a new and refreshing outlook and stimulated his jaded intellect. She was eager to learn and he was willing to teach.

Sarah loved and admired Thomas: she tried to model herself on Louise for she longed to be like her and wished she knew the secret of that calm serenity, that peace of mind and quiet contentment. For she was often discontented, wanting something she could not define, impatient with childhood and avid for maturity.

She seldom saw the hoyden Ann but she learned the things to avoid for she was convinced that no man could ever tolerate the rebellious and mischievous high spirits, the laughing disregard for convention, the keen enjoyment of life.

One grievance which flamed in her youthful being was her brother's staunch refusal to allow her to attend his parties. He tried to point out that she was too young to mingle with his friends who would be constrained by her presence. They might pretend amusement and indulgence but they would resent the necessary guard on their conversation and behaviour.

Thomas decided to give a party to celebrate Louise's seventeenth birthday. Sarah pleaded to be allowed to attend and when she indulged in passionate tears, he relented enough to promise that she could come to the house if she would stay in an adjoining room.

She could watch the guests arriving: she would be able to hear the music and watch the dancing; and she could enjoy the many delicacies he meant to provide for his guests.

When the evening came, she took up her position behind the door of the little room, craning excitedly to watch the crush of arriving guests. The big hall was a blaze of light and Sarah caught her breath again and again at the dazzling richness of a gown, the beauty of a woman in sparkling jewels and bright gown, the immaculate good looks of their escorts. There was a sickness at the pit of her stomach and her throat ached with the tears of excitement. How she longed to be grown up, to wear a rich velvet gown with diamonds in her ears and hair and at her throat! To walk into a house on a man's arm and bask in the adoration of his gaze! To be greeted warmly by friends and to drink champagne and eat the delectable food which had been laid out in readiness.

Louise moved forward to greet a new arrival. She was all in white and rich garnets were about her creamy throat. Her dark hair was smooth and neat, piled high on her head. How dainty she was, how slim and elegant, how self-possessed! Then Sarah stared her surprise . . . for Martin took Louise's hands in both of his own and smiled down at her with warmth and affection. Sarah could not mistake the tall, lean frame, the graceful movements, the breadth of the shoulders and the set of that proud, dark head. It was Martin — whom she had believed to be in Paris. It was all she could do not to run out eagerly to greet him. For so many years, she had thought of him as her brother and loved him dearly: now she thought of him not only as a cousin but as a much-loved and familiar friend. She missed him when he was away and looked forward to the occasional letter or postcard from Paris or Rome, Copenhagen or Berlin. He had never treated her as a child but always as an equal and with him, she did not remember that she was a child. The fifteen years between their ages did not seem important.

She willed him to glance in her direction. Louise spoke to him, smiling, and then he looked towards the door swiftly. Like a shy and timid baby, she drew back — and then peeped again. He lifted a hand in brief salute and smiled.

"I should think everyone must be intrigued by the golden-haired fairy who stands watching them arrive," he said to Louise.

She smiled. "She has promised to be discreet and not to make her presence obvious. I expect she's longing to speak to you."

"Oh, I won't neglect her," he promised. "I'll keep her company for a little while."

"Not now, Martin," she said quickly. "You must come and meet some people." And she took his arm and guided him towards the big, bright, noisy room. "You look very well, Martin. Are you home now for some time?"

"For a few months. I prefer to live abroad, though. The climate suits me — I hate English weather."

She looked up at him mischievously. "You'll bring home a foreign wife one day, I expect."

He smiled. "I'll never find a girl in any country to match you for looks and charm, Louise," he said gallantly, and she coloured prettily at the compliment.

They talked for a few minutes. Then Martin said: "There's Marchmont. I didn't know that Thomas knew him."

"Thomas knows so many people," she replied easily.

The man he had mentioned excused himself from his companions and threaded his way through the crowd to reach them. "I thought you were still in Paris, Fallow," he said lightly. His glance swept approvingly over Louise's white slimness and piquantly lovely face.

"You know my cousin, Louise Fallow, of course," Martin said.

"No, I've not had the pleasure of meeting Miss Fallow," he returned, smiling.

Martin made the introduction: "Louise, this is George Marchmont . . . Veerham's younger son. We were at Cambridge together."

George gave a mock sigh. "The younger son — and doomed to be penniless, I'm afraid. I can only hope that my charms, such as they are, will win me a wife with a fortune."

Louise laughed. Her pleasant, musical laughter reached her brother's ears and he turned to smile across the room — a brotherly, indulgent and affectionate smile.

Martin looked about the room. "Excuse me, Louise — I must have a word with my father. He's with Colonel Grainger, the worst bore of his Club, and I ought to rescue him. I'll leave you in George's care," he added lightly. "He talks too much but is perfectly harmless." With this parting sally, he left them.

They exchanged amused yet slightly shy glances. "May I get you a drink?" he asked diffidently.

"No, thank you. But I think I'd like to sit for a few minutes."

He guided her across the room to a vacant seat. He stood by her side, watching the dancers, nodding or smiling in reply to passing remarks from people he knew. She looked up at him shyly. "This is a crush, isn't it? Thomas always gives such popular parties."

He smiled at her. "Aren't you his sister?"

She nodded. "Yes."

"I thought you must be." He grinned suddenly, mischievously. "I say, isn't it true that you're a pretty wealthy family, Louise? You might be the answer to my problems."

She was taken aback . . . then as she met his dancing, merry eyes, she realized that he was joking. She smiled, a little hesitantly. "Oh, but I have two sisters . . . much prettier."

"Poor Cinderella," he teased. "Will you leave your slipper when you vanish at the stroke of midnight? I hope you mean to let me have your address so I can find you again." He took her hand and pressed her fingers gently, meaningly, in the manner of the accomplished flirt. "Who could be interested in your sisters once they've met you?" he said softly.

Louise was a little frightened by his manner of conversation, by the bold admiration of his glance and words — but she found him amusing and somewhat likeable and almost hoped that he might come to mean his bantering words. She was naturally shy and reticent and there was something in her air of quiet dignity and slight aloofness that prevented most men from flirting with her although she met many young men at the parties so loved by Thomas and through the subtle manoeuvres of her aunt. George

Marchmont's easy address and casual charm was almost new to her — and she was young and impressionable enough to be flattered and somewhat excited by his attentions throughout the evening . . .

The following summer, she married George. Despite the rumour that Bernice St. Clair had manoeuvred the marriage, it was a love match and nothing else. George was definitely not the penniless young man he had represented himself to be — but Louise would have married him, anyway, so happy, so proud, so dazed was she that he had evidently fallen in love with her.

He was a warm-hearted, generous and kind young man and Louise found his sense of humour one of his nicest and most appealing traits.

Their courtship had not been smooth and easy-flowing. Louise knew that she had fallen in love with him but she was too shy, too humble, to believe that he could mean anything but flirtation so she tried to avoid him, refused many of his invitations, pretended to be out when he called at the St. Clair house and endeavoured to encourage the attentions of other men to prove that she was not a country girl who knew nothing of sophistry but an experienced young woman in affairs of the heart.

George was not deceived. He was a single-minded man and he had decided to marry Louise Fallow at their first meeting. He called on Lady St. Clair and asked for her advice. He neither expected nor received discouragement for he was an eligible bachelor and Bernice was delighted to realize that his intentions were serious and honourable.

She subtly persuaded Louise to accept his invitations, to join theatre parties which included George as a guest, to be gracious and charming to him, to dine and dance and drive with him, to send little notes of thanks when he sent flowers or books. And she told Louise firmly that if she was fond of George and hoped to marry him, then she should allow him to recognize the fact for he would not be patient for ever.

The next time George called, Louise said abruptly and impulsively: "Aunt Bernice tells me that you want to marry me."

He almost choked on the excellent coffee she had poured for him. Her direct words took him by surprise. But he set down his cup, wiped his mouth slowly and carefully, and said with a smile: "Yes, that's right. I told you that I was in search of a wealthy wife to save me from starvation."

As usual, he met seriousness with levity and was rewarded by her light laugh. "Isn't that rather a drastic step?" she teased. "You scarcely know me, George — and besides, it isn't true that you're the penniless younger son."

He gave a little, helpless gesture. "My secret is out!" he exclaimed dramatically. "And I hoped you would be sorry for me. I can't think of any other reason to ask you to marry me."

She looked at him steadily. "I think that's a very weak reason, anyway, George."

He rose and came to sit beside her on the couch. He took her hand and held it to his cheek. "Is love a better reason? I love you, Louise — and I wish you'd marry me." He sounded little more than a boy in that moment, so urgent, so impulsive was the appeal. "I'd try to make you happy," he added earnestly.

"Would you make a good husband?" she teased him. "I have a long list of qualities I most admire in men."

"What are they?" he demanded.

"Well . . . I don't like men who drink too much," she said quietly.

He coloured slightly, wondering if Martin had told her of their Cambridge days and his own weak head where alcohol was concerned. "I hope you would never see me the worse for drink," he said fervently. "And I don't gamble," he went on hopefully. "I'm not interested in other women . . . not since I met you. And I do love you . . . " he said in a rush.

Her eyes melted with warmth. "Oh, I shouldn't tease you," she said repentantly. "Of course I'll marry you, George."

He took her into his arms and held her close but his embrace was tender and considerate. "Oh, Louise . . . will you really marry me?"

Louise nodded. "Yes, please," she said shyly and kissed him, secure in the knowledge that they would be happy and that she could not wish for anyone nicer, kinder or more worthy of her love than George Marchmont . . .

She was married from the St. Clair house at St. George's, Hanover Square — "a good omen!" declared her bridegroom confidently — and she was radiantly lovely in white satin with the lace veil which had been worn by generations of St. Clair brides. A flushed and almost inarticulate George stumbled his way through the ceremony, overcome by shyness, embarrassment and his good fortune — but when it was over and he drove with Louise to the reception, he assured her that he wouldn't have gone through that awful ordeal for anyone else — and wasn't that proof of his love for her?

It was a fashionable and well-attended wedding. Thomas was distinguished and handsome and certainly at his most charming. Her bridesmaids, Ann, Sarah and four of George's cousins, were like a bouquet of flowers in their colourful prettiness. The reception was on a grand scale and champagne flowed lavishly. The young couple left early for their honeymoon in Paris but the festivities went on long after their departure.

Sarah was a little sad. The excitement of the day was mingled with a sense of loss now that Louise was married. She was jealous of her sister's affections and if she had not been so fond of George, she felt sure she would dislike him. Louise's marriage seemed like the knell of doom to the thirteen year old Sarah — the first of many changes. Louise would no longer welcome her when she went to stay with the St. Clairs. They would no longer enjoy long, intimate talks. She would miss the steadying, demure influence of Louise over her own more excitable and temperamental nature. They would not go together to the studio and know the mutual affection and intimacy under the roof of the house where all of them had been born.

George and Louise were to live on one of the Veerham estates and although they would be often in London, Sarah gloomily felt that there would be no place for her in her sister's life in the future.

It occurred to her that Thomas was twenty-three and might be the next to marry — and then she would lose him too. They were the two people she loved best. She loved the couple who had always been father and mother to her, of course; they were always so good and kind and loving — but she was not attuned to them as she was to Thomas and Louise. They did not understand her odd precocity, the maturity of her thoughts and feelings, her hunger for knowledge and the longing to be treated as an adult.

Martin was the only other person who tried to understand and did not treat her like an ignorant child. But Martin was, as usual, abroad and she wondered why he so seldom stayed in England for more than two or three months at a time. He was almost a stranger these days — except that he could never be a stranger to her. She loved him too much . . . but she was angry with him in a way that she could not define. He should not be abroad when she needed him. Why had he not made the effort to attend the wedding? He had introduced Louise to George, after all . . .

Sarah returned to The Meads the following day. Her studies had been much neglected of recent weeks and now she threw herself eagerly into her lessons. Her governess, Miss Lake, was in her late twenties; clever and capable, she had the gift of instilling knowledge with seemingly little effort. She taught in subtle ways: she encouraged Sarah to ask questions and she applauded her love of reading; she found Sarah an apt pupil with a ready talent for sketching, a gift for languages, a pleasant touch on the piano and application for sewing. She had a musical singing voice and a ready wit: an inborn grace of movement, an instinctive flair for clothes, a natural beauty and a readiness to please. Miss Lake, who had been at The Meads for two years, was confident that the child would become an attractive young woman with an ease of manner and a pleasing personality.

Sarah liked and admired her governess. She was eager to please the young woman with the twinkling grey eyes and whimsical mouth. Sarah was particularly interested in Miss Lake's skill with water colours. They were cleverly done and really delightful, fresh and delicate. Her sketches were lifelike and full of character. Sarah decided that Thomas should be encouraged to take an interest and she concerned herself with ways and means. She knew, with her odd instinct for knowing such things, that Miss Lake was not particularly well paid; she was always neatly dressed and she had been well educated; but Sarah felt that she could not have private means or she would never have chosen to teach the children of strangers.

She frequently talked about her brother. One day, Miss Lake admitted that she had visited his last exhibition.

"Tell me what you think of his work!" Sarah urged.

Miss Lake paused. "I'm not an expert on art."

"But you have an opinion," Sarah said impatiently.

"I think he's very clever." She sighed briefly. "I wish I had a little of his talent."

"Did you understand his paintings?"

Miss Lake smiled faintly. "Yes. I know that many people are bewildered by them but I do presume to believe that I understand them."

"Thomas would be so pleased," Sarah said eagerly. "And I think he'd like to see your sketches one day. I shall invite him to tea one day — and you must promise to show him your book."

"My dear child!" she exclaimed but her cheeks were touched with colour. "Your brother wouldn't come all this way just to see my sketches — and I wouldn't dream of boring him, Sarah." She bent her head over the atlas on the table. "Come along . . . we've talked enough and this is supposed to be your geography lesson."

Obediently Sarah began to study her own atlas — but she was determined to carry out her suggestion. Thomas would think nothing of the journey from London . . .

It was a warm afternoon and Sarah's

golden head was bowed over a book in her lap as she sat on the grass. Miss Lake had forgotten her charge: the heat of the afternoon; everything but her sketch of the village church nestling on the hill among heavily-wooded countryside.

Thomas stood by the gate, unobserved. As he walked along the quiet lane to the house, he had caught the glint of sun-touched gold from Sarah's hair.

He liked the look of the neat, slender governess. The look of avid concentration did not detract from the attractive lineage of her small face: her rich brown hair was neatly coiled on the nape of her neck — and Thomas knew instinctively that it would fall in a heavy mass to her waist if it was loosened and the desire rose in him to loosen it; the silver grey of her dress fell becomingly about her slim figure — yet despite her air of demurity he felt that there was a repressed vitality and strength of character, a quick wit and a sense of humour, perception and understanding. He scarcely looked at Sarah. His gaze fell solely on the woman and he was reluctant to make his presence known for then she would guard her expressions — and at the moment her face was a joy to him. The swift annoyance when a line would not come right: the instant pleasure that radiated when she captured an elusive fragment of the scene; the keen interest and complete absorption.

Sarah was engrossed in her book — but she sensed his presence and looked up. Within a second the book was thrown aside and she was on her feet. "Thomas! You did come! Why stand there like a man in a dream? Come and meet Miss Lake."

He allowed Sarah to draw him forward, realizing that her words had struck home. He *had* been a man in a dream — his only companion this lovely creature whose expression was now startled and shy.

Sarah introduced them and then stood watching them both, her face bright as if she triumphed that she had brought about the meeting unknown to Miss Lake.

Thomas took the woman's hand and clasped it firmly. His bright blue eyes gazed deeply into hers as though he assured her that there need be no shyness between them. Her cheeks were still pink and she stood with her hand in his, oddly unsure of herself, oddly bewildered by a flood of emotion that swept through her as their eyes met. Her hand was cool and slightly tremulous in his grasp and he longed to slip his arm about her shoulders and talk gently to her. The instinct to protect others had always been strong in him . . . now it was fully aroused . . .

★ ★ ★

Robert flashed his nephew a glance as though he doubted his sanity. "But, Thomas, you can't be serious!" he protested.

Thomas smiled coolly and Robert

felt at a disadvantage. Thomas had always had the knack of putting him in his place . . . he was so calm and self-possessed, so arrogantly sure of himself. He had a strong will and it was foolish to gainsay him. Looking now at that determined chin, the set of his head and the unconcern in his blue eyes, Robert felt it would gain him nothing to argue . . . yet it was his duty to endeavour to drum some sense into him.

"Oh, I suppose you are," he went on irritably. "But you scarcely know the girl — and don't you know what people will say! For a man in your position . . . well, frankly, Thomas, you don't have to marry a governess, you know! I'm sure you could take your pick from a dozen girls — girls of good family with money behind them!"

"Don't be snobbish, Uncle Bob. Mariana is worth a dozen of those girls — and I might add that I'm bored to tears with girls of good family with money behind them. Mariana has brains as well as looks. Do you think I care that she has to earn her living as a governess at the moment? She'll never need to do so again. I tell you, Uncle Bob, she has more charm and grace and sweetness than any of those girls whose fond mothers would gladly welcome me as a son-in-law."

"Well, consider Miss Lake — if nothing else." Robert tried a different tack. "Do you think she'll be happy with you? Do you think she can settle in to your way of life — and you must admit that it's a little eccentric? Will she enjoy being snubbed and humiliated by those society girls who seem to frequent your house? She knows that she isn't a member of our class — and I'm sure she'll know better than to marry into it!"

His nephew's expression was suddenly grim. He said curtly: "Antiquated rubbish! I shall know how to deal with anyone who snubs or humiliates my wife! Mariana and I are engaged — and there's an end to it!"

Robert rushed in: "Why not go abroad for a while, Thomas? Think it over — don't do anything hasty. An engagement doesn't really mean very much, does it? You could join Martin in Austria . . . find new subjects for your work. Miss Lake will believe that you've thought better of your so-called engagement. I'll dismiss her and you need never set eyes on her again . . . you're young, impulsive — I know how these things happen . . . "

Thomas interrupted him and his tone was icy. "I'll do nothing of the kind. What kind of a man do you think I am? I happen to love Mariana — and she loves me!"

There was a dismal silence. Then Robert said, still with a vestige of hope: "You really mean to marry her — or is this just another affair?"

"I mean to marry her." His tone was final.

"And nothing I say will make you change your mind, I suppose?"

"Nothing at all. Mariana and I will

be married as soon as possible."

Admitting defeat, Robert rose and crossed to the decanters. He carefully poured brandy into two glasses and handed one to Thomas. "Your very good health," he said absently. Then he smiled and said graciously: "I hope your marriage will be as happy and successful as mine, my boy." He sat down again and regarded his nephew thoughtfully. He was a man and old enough to make his own decisions yet Robert wished he had not chosen Mariana Lake for a wife. She was respectful, neat and intelligent: pleasant-spoken and quiet with the happy knack of effacing herself when necessary; Sarah was devoted to the woman. But Robert's liking and admiration were not sufficient to accept the thought of Mariana Lake as a member of the family . . .

Thomas swirled the brandy in his glass. His mouth was set firmly. He said abruptly: "I wish I could make you understand that this isn't a boyish impulse but a very real love on both sides. I loved Mariana the first time I saw her here — two years ago. You think that we scarcely know each other because we've met so seldom. We've always known each other, Uncle Bob — and our infrequent meetings are not my fault. Mariana thought as you do at first . . . that I should marry a wealthy girl, a girl of my own class — at other times she said that artists should never marry, that love and marriage would only interfere with my work. I asked her five times to marry me." He smiled ruefully. "Don't you think it's unfair that a man's name and income and success should be held against him — for those were Mariana's arguments. My name doesn't mean a thing unless she shares it. My income merely means that we can both live in comfort and provide for any children that we have. My success . . . doesn't mean a thing to me — I paint for the sheer joy of painting and it isn't my fault that people choose to deck their homes out with my work."

Robert shook his head dubiously. "Thomas, I've given my blessing . . . you needn't press these persuasive arguments on me. You're twenty-five — a grown man. I have no jurisdiction over you. If you choose to marry Miss Lake then I can't prevent you. I can only hope that you never regret it." He added quietly: "She's some years older than you, Thomas . . . you don't consider that a drawback?"

Thomas laughed. "My dear uncle, when has age ever been a primary consideration in marriage? You're right, Mariana is older than me . . . but only by a few years. I love her — and I know we can be happy together. We have similar interests. She understands my work and encourages me. I respect and admire her intelligence and her strength of character. I've no fears for my future . . . I hope that Mariana hasn't any. To be sure, I'm getting the best bargain!"

"You realize that your friends will consider it a very eccentric marriage?"

"Oh, nonsense! It would be the height of absurd eccentricity to tie myself to a simpering, inane girl whom I couldn't possibly care for. I love my Mariana dearly — and nothing will prevent me from marrying her . . . "

Sarah was delighted with the news. She had decided long before that Thomas should marry her governess, having brought about their first meeting and having continually impressed on Miss Lake what a fine, upstanding person he was, how kind, how good, how understanding. She had noted the swift flush that touched the woman's cheek at the mention of her brother, how bright were her eyes when he came to The Meads, how quickly she lowered her gaze to conceal the warm regard, how swiftly she hushed her charge when the girl's tongue almost ran away with her and she was on the point of telling Thomas how often he appeared in Miss Lake's sketches, how frequently she asked questions about him and how glad she was when he came to The Meads on a brief visit.

And Mariana Lake? Loving him almost against her will, against the common-sense arguments of her brain, yet she had never encouraged him. Her greetings had always been coolly friendly: her remarks light and conversational; she avoided being alone with him and checked any tendency on his part towards affectionate conversation. If he came unexpectedly to find her alone in the garden or the house, she bustled away to find Sarah — always allowing Thomas to believe that she thought he came to see his little sister.

But Sarah, at fifteen, could scarcely be called his 'little' sister. She was tall and slender: her figure showed signs of maturity; her golden hair no longer fell to her waist but was coiled neatly on her neck. She was growing up yet to the impatient girl it still seemed an eternity until she could take her place as an adult in the world. She knew that her intellect was that of a mature woman: her body certainly was; her spirit had never been that of a child. But to the world she was but fifteen . . .

But if Miss Lake was going to marry Thomas, then perhaps there would be no more lessons. Surely her uncle would not engage a new governess for the remainder of her education?

She was glad that Thomas was going to be married. She did not dread the changes that the years brought any longer. She could laugh at the child she had been when Louise married George and it seemed that her small world was being turned upside down. She realised now that these things were inevitable: birth, marriage, procreation and death. One day she would marry and have children. Then, when she was an old, old woman, she would die. She did not worry about the latter fate — for old age and death seemed much too far away . . .

With the wedding on everyone's mind, Sarah's thoughts turned to romance. Then she began to think about her parents. She had been told the story of her mother's death on her birth: her father's remarriage and the tragic accident in France. In very much the same way as the small Thomas, she considered her status as an orphan and it seemed both pathetic and romantic to her mind. For a few days, she swept about the house, acting as heavily and as dramatically as any tragedy queen until, with a few well-chosen words, Mariana Lake pointed out that the orphan state was not a pleasant one, that she was very fortunate to have been adopted by so kind, charming and indulgent an uncle and aunt, that many orphans went to institutions and were then forced to earn their living and had no one to give them affection and kindness.

Thomas was thankful that Mariana agreed with him on a quiet wedding. They were married from The Meads at the small village church. With an impulsive kindness, Robert offered to give the bride away when he learned that she had no parents or other family.

Martin came from Austria to play the part of best man and Sarah was the only bridesmaid. She was an excellent foil to Mariana's dark attractions with her golden beauty. No one could call Mariana beautiful but her dark eyes and sweet face and generous, whimsical mouth had their own appeal — and to Thomas she was the loveliest woman in the world as she came shyly down the aisle on his uncle's arm.

Few of the family attended the ceremony. Ann was at school in Switzerland. Louise was expecting her first child and George would not leave her side, so lovingly anxious was he for her health. Bernice St. Clair came in sombre black for her husband had recently died. Thomas had invited only one or two of his closest friends — and Mariana had no one she wished to invite.

Martin seemed a very handsome figure to Sarah. She saw him so seldom that her heart leaped with excitement whenever he came to England. He had the power to embarrass her and to still her usually-active tongue. Shyness engulfed her when he was with her — and when she remembered that he had been almost a brother to her all her life she thought herself foolish and childish.

She studied him discreetly but intently. He was thirty years old and little grey strands streaked his temples. A few lines were etched about his eyes and he looked weary. Sarah wondered why he always lived abroad. She wondered too that he had never married — and at the thought of his possible marriage one day she was filled with a violent, painful emotion. Tears welled within her heart — and hastily she turned to Aunt Bernice and began to talk of anything that entered her head. Her aunt was growing a little short-sighted and did not notice the sudden, shocking ravages of emotion in Sarah's youthful face. It occurred to her that the child's voice was too high-pitched and that her manner was slightly odd — but she attributed these things to the excitement of her brother's wedding.

As for Martin, it occurred to him that Sarah was no longer a child. It seemed strange and a little unwelcome . . . this realization that she was growing into a lovely woman. He found himself admiring her loveliness, her tiny waist and well-rounded figure: she was so coolly self-assured and so adult in her conversation and manner that he found it difficult to remember that she was, after all, little more than a child. But a captivating, enchanting child in her rose pink dress and the wreath of roses in her golden hair, her cheeks flushed with excitement and her eyes seemingly brighter and of a more vivid blue than he had ever known.

When he returned to Austria, some days later, it was this memory of her he carried with him . . . and also a promise from Sarah that she would gladly write to him if he diligently and faithfully wrote in reply.

3

SARAH swept into the big, pleasant nursery, stripping off her gloves. Her golden hair was piled into a startling coronet on her proud head, her slim figure was encased in a smart suit of deep green and her loveliness held that rare quality of true sweetness and purity within.

"My dear Louise, whenever I come here, you're always to be found in the nursery!" she exclaimed, laughing — but there was a hint of rebuke behind the careless words.

Smiling, Louise added another brick to the imposing structure that she was erecting for the amusement of her youngest child, Lionel, who was two years old. At the table sat Lucy, five years old, diligently employed in covering a sheet of drawing paper with vivid paints.

"Can you tell me a better place for me to spend my time?" she returned mildly. "My children are entitled to know their mother. Our mother spent a brief hour or so every day in the nursery — and it was never enough. But Aunt Bernice devoted as much time as she could to being with us, reading to us, playing with us, taking us out for picnics and walks and to the coast. It's very important to children to feel secure and loved, to feel that grown-ups are not too busy or too bored to give their time to them. I'm determined that my children shall have as much of my time as they wish."

Sarah looked at Louise with shrewd eyes. She sat down at the table and put an arm about Lucy, pressing a kiss to the smooth, rounded, satin-soft cheek. The child shrugged away from the caress and applied herself with concentration to her daubs.

Sarah laughed. "We have another artist in the family," she said lightly.

Louise, not caring that as fast as

she piled the bricks, Lionel knocked them to the floor, was still busy with the building of the imposing edifice. "Thomas encourages her," she returned absently. "I can't stop her playing with those messy paints. What *do* you think of that ridiculous box of paints? It's much too old for her — but Thomas would insist that she have them. They're ruined already." She gave a little sigh. "She doesn't seem to be interested in dolls or books or toys . . . just paint and paper. And if I try to take them away, she screams at the top of her voice. Just like Ann when she was a child — strong-willed."

Sarah looked up from her study of Lucy's painting. "How is Ann? Have you heard from her lately?"

Louise met her eyes cooly and serenely. "Have you?"

Sarah shook her head. "Heavens, no! Ann never writes to me — we have nothing in common! Is she still living with that impossible man in Rome?"

Louise nodded. "As far as I know.

145

What on earth possesseed her, Sarah? Everyone is talking about the affair — and it makes me very uncomfortable. After all, she is my sister and I think she's behaved disgracefully — but am I supposed to say so or should I try to defend her?" She sighed again. "I'm sure I don't know."

Sarah shrugged. "It was a silly thing to do, Louise — but not really such a disgrace, after all. If she's happy then that's all that matters, don't you think?"

"Perhaps it doesn't seem so bad to you," Louise said tartly. "But I think it's a shocking business. George has forbidden me to write to her or to see her again — he says that to have such a woman in the house would be a bad influence for the children. And I'm inclined to agree even if Ann is my sister."

Sarah thought that George's own morals would not bear close scrutiny but it was typical of the man to condemn the immoral behaviour of others. She was too wise to speak her thoughts. Even if Louise knew of her husband's affairs with other women, she would never admit it to anyone and Sarah thought it very likely that she would refuse to listen to the most convincing evidence of his infidelity. Sarah did not wholly blame George. Louise was completely engrossed in her children and relegated her husband to the background. He was not a man to find happiness in domestic affairs and Sarah suspected that he was bored with a wife who talked of nothing but housekeeping and the health and interests of the children.

She said shortly: "I don't know that I blame Ann very much. I'd have hated to be married to Vincent Riley too — no doubt I'd have taken the first opportunity to go away with another man."

Louise threw her a shocked, incredulous glance. "That's a very young and silly remark to make, Sarah. Marriage is a sacred pledge between two people. If we countenance the breaking of sacred vows, then we're no longer respectable and decent-thinking people."

"My dear Louise, you're pathetically out of date with your views," Sarah said wearily. "I believe that if two people are incompatible or unhappy, then they shouldn't go on living together. Divorce is the only solution — and it does give them both a second chance of happiness."

Louise stared at her in amazement. Sarah had never spoken so bluntly on the subject before although she had hinted that she did not find Ann's elopement with Freddie Hastings so terrible.

"Vince will never divorce Ann," she said firmly.

"More fool he," Sarah said, bored with the subject.

"He still loves Ann very much — and I think he's right not to divorce her. She'll get tired of that man eventually and be only too glad to go back to her husband."

"And he'll welcome her with open arms, I suppose," Sarah said dryly.

"Well . . . not exactly. One wouldn't expect him to be that generous and charitable. But I expect he will take her back and when she has proved that she is really repentant, then he will relent towards her."

"A delightful prospect. I expect Ann knows what he would be like — stuffy, pompous old bore! I can't see her running back to fall on her knees and beg for forgiveness. Anyway, if he really cared for Ann, he would give her the freedom she obviously wants. Living with the man you love is all very well for a time . . . but it doesn't offer the security and peace of mind of marriage."

"I doubt if that worries Ann unduly," Louise said tartly. "She never did care much for conventions. And when that man tires of her she'll probably find herself another lover." Abruptly she noticed that Lucy was listening avidly. "We shouldn't discuss such things

149

before the children," she said coldly. "They're so quick to repeat things."

"Oh, they're much too young to understand," Sarah said carelessly. She rose and stretched her lithe, young body with indolent sensuality. "Let's go down, Louise. I'm dying for some tea. I've been into the country with Alan Fitzgerald and I'm parched."

Reluctantly, Louise left the children with the strict injunction to Lucy to look after her little brother until Nanny came, and accompanied her sister down the wide staircase, talking eagerly and indulgently of her children. Sarah felt very bored and sympathized with George if Louise always carried on in that vein. Children were lovable and sweet, when they were good, but there were other things in life, she thought with faint scorn. She wondered, not for the first time, when Louise had strayed from being a quiet, intelligent and attractive young woman with a keen grasp of world affairs. No doubt George had appreciated her intelligence and swift understanding and warmly affectionate nature. But, since Lucy's birth, Louise had become like a broody hen with one chick and her world had dwindled steadily until it revolved only about herself and the children.

Tea was brought and as Louise rose to fetch a small trinket which George had given to her on the previous day, Sarah's eyes sharpened. "You're getting plump. You aren't pregnant again, are you?" She did not realize the faint emphasis on that 'again' or the irritability of her tone.

Louise coloured slightly. "Do you have to be so blunt, Sarah?"

"Well, are you? Of course you are — that colour in your cheeks is my answer. What does George think about it?"

Her sister's expression held a faint distaste for Sarah's inquisitive remark. She resented the implication that George did not welcome another child — and she resented Sarah's prying into the intimate affairs of her marriage.

"He's delighted, of course," she said firmly. "We hoped for a big family."

"No doubt you did," Sarah said dryly . . . and Louise knew that she had not included George in her comment.

She changed the subject hastily. "Did you say that you've been with Alan Fitzgerald? You seem to be seeing a lot of him, Sarah."

"Why not?" She mocked the tentative hope in her sister's tone.

"Isn't he rather a dangerous young man, darling? I mean . . . well, he hasn't a very nice reputation. I should hate you to be talked about — and you must admit that he's courted a great many girls without marrying them." She lowered her voice slightly as she went on: "And there was that scandal about the Dearham girl."

"Her baby, you mean?" Sarah said bluntly. "Oh, I don't hold that against him. She should have known better. I rather like Alan . . . he's amusing and intelligent — and I rather enjoy keeping him at arms' length, you know.

As for being talked about . . . well, I don't much care what people think, Louise."

"But you have been out with him a great deal lately."

Sarah chuckled softly. "You needn't look so hopeful, Louise. I'm not going to marry him — and he *has* asked me." She laughed again. "It must be the first time that Alan has ever proposed — and I don't think he believes that I'm not interested in marrying him. It's a frightful blow to his pride."

She knew that Louise wanted her to marry and settle down, that she was always hoping for the announcement of her engagement to one or other of her many men-friends. But Sarah was not really interested in any of them except as friends. She carried an ideal in her heart — and she had not yet found any man to compare with it. She liked the boyish, attentive and eager to please young men who sought her company — but she had no wish to marry any of them. It pleased her to dine with them, to dance and flirt a little, to drive to the coast or into the country, to go to theatres and parties, to attend Ascot and Wimbledon with an eligible, handsome escort. She had unconventional ideas and she was very interested in subjects that men did not care for her to know about. But they chose to overlook this sign of eccentricity, each confident that marriage would mould her into a conformable, conventional and pleasing wife. She flirted dexterously and had become adroit at assuring ambitious men that she was very fond of them but could not marry them in all fairness to their affection for her.

She suddenly gave a sharp exclamation. "I've a shocking memory! I've just remembered why I asked Alan to drop me outside your door . . . did you have a letter from Thomas?"

"Last week," Louise replied with a slight frown.

"Yes, so did I. What did you think of their news?"

Louise shrugged. "I can't understand why he wants to live in Italy," she said coldly. "Isn't England good enough for them?"

"But, Louise, you don't understand! An artist needs a warm climate and colourful surroundings. How anyone ever expects an artist to produce good work in this cold, damp climate, I shall never know!"

"Cold and damp it may be but English children are the healthiest in the world — and I should have thought that their first consideration would be for their child. I don't know what his wife is thinking of to agree to such a wild scheme. But what can you expect of a woman of that class?" Her tone and manner were contemptuous.

Sarah rose swiftly, anger flooding through her. "How unpleasant you can be!" she snapped. "You never used to be such a snob — and Mariana is as good as either of us. I think she's wonderful . . . sweet and lovable and very intelligent — and I'm only too pleased to claim her as a sister!"

Louise was flushed and hurt. On the point of returning a sharp retort, utterly alien to her nature and her belief in turning the other cheek, she checked the words as the door opened and their cousin came into the room.

They both turned and Sarah was the first to exclaim, with shining eyes: "Martin! What a lovely surprise!" Then, regaining her self-possession, she added: "You've arrived in time to avert a disaster." She turned to Louise with an affectionately warm smile. "I'm sorry, darling . . . I didn't mean to be rude. I'm afraid I lost my temper."

Louise gestured vaguely and then Martin came forward to kiss her cheek. "You're looking very well — and very pretty these days," he said. "How's George and the children?" She coloured at the compliment but assured him that everyone was well and went on to regale him with Lionel's latest achievements and Lucy's prowess at the small private school she attended. He listened with seeming interest and pleasing courtesy and when she finished he turned to Sarah, taking her hands and pressing them firmly. "As lovely as ever . . . I've just been listening to a diatribe on your virtues from Alan Fitzgerald. I met him at the Club and learned that he'd dropped you here. So I'm killing two birds with one stone . . . seeing you both at the same time."

He sat down and accepted tea from Louise and kept them amused for the next half-hour with his light and easy conversation.

Sarah laughed and talked easily and without conscious desire to charm. But she was very aware of this tall, attractive man with his lean sculptured and sensitive face. It seemed impossible now to remember that he had once seemed a brother to her — no brother could stir the blood in her veins or quicken her heartbeat or fill her with acute and passionate yearning as this man did.

His mother had died two years ago and since that day, Robert Fallow had lost all interest in business affairs and his once-active social life. He now led a solitary and lonely life at The Meads for Sarah was mostly in London and Martin continued to travel all over Europe. Sarah stayed at the family house at Thomas' suggestion. Not knowing when, if ever, he would return to England to live but feeling that the house should be kept in readiness for him if he ever decided to pay a brief visit to London, he had asked Sarah to use it as her home whenever she wished. Realizing that her uncle's health and spirits were broken by the death of his wife and, sympathetic though she was, feeling that her own spirit would be cramped and stifled in the atmosphere of mourning, she had readily agreed. Robert had not objected: he merely wished to be left alone to mourn for Elizabeth. His only stipulation was that Sarah should have an elderly, respectable woman to live with her as companion and chaperone.

Sarah had made her own choice of

companion and the 'elderly, respectable woman' was only a few years older than herself, a pleasant and well-spoken girl who had originally been employed by Louise as nurse to the children. George's roving eye had found her within a very short space of time and Louise had dismissed her peremptorily when she learned that the girl was expecting a child. If she knew or suspected that George was responsible for the girl's condition, she did not betray her knowledge or suspicion.

Sarah had made it her business to trace the girl. She discovered her living in a mean house in a poor district with very little money. She had taken a liking to the girl, admiring her unbroken spirit and proud heart. She had asked her to live with her as a companion and friend and assured her that her child would be welcome. Louise never spoke of the girl or her child and Sarah, for the sake of tact and kindness, was careful never to mention the name of Cathryn Manners.

Many people condemned her for helping Cathryn: her men-friends reluctantly approved her eagerness to help someone less fortunate than herself but privately thought that her quixotic impulses would need to be checked; no one dared to hint that the little boy might be Sarah's own child by some unknown man. It was said of Sarah Fallow that she did not give a damn for the opinion or remarks of others. If she set her mind on a particular course of action she would follow it to the bitter end. She had a scathing tongue and did not hesitate to turn it upon her critics. Many an outspoken person turned away with burning cheeks and angry heart after being attacked for their lack of charity and their readiness to condemn a girl for one mistake.

The identity of Daniel's father was commonly known — and only Louise apparently refused to admit the truth. Sarah had tackled George herself on the subject of maintenance for Cathryn and the child — and incurred his lasting dislike and enmity. He had sullenly agreed to support them both to a certain extent with the proviso that Sarah would not tell Louise anything about the arrangement. They had not met since that day for Sarah only called on Louise when George was out or away from home. If they met in the street or at a social function, she ignored him if he was alone, was icily and formally courteous if Louise accompanied him. Louise did not seem to notice their mutual reluctance to meet or their lack of friendliness towards each other — or else, Sarah decided, she knew the truth and guessed at the reason for their abrupt hostility.

At last, Sarah rose. "I must be going," she said lightly. "I'm going to a party this evening. Thank you for the tea, Louise. Give my regards to George, won't you — and tell him that I'm sorry to have missed him." Her voice was touched with a deceptive sweetness.

Martin glanced at his watch and also

got to his feet. "My car's outside. Can I give you a lift, Sarah?"

She smiled at him. "Thank you . . . I should be grateful. It's impossible to get a taxi at this time of the day."

They talked idly as he drove carefully and with enforced slowness through the heavy stream of traffic. She glanced at him occasionally through the thick veil of her lashes and thought how handsome he was in his quiet, rather distinguished way. Thomas was a handsome man but his good looks were flamboyant and slightly extravagant. Perhaps Martin's claim was more to attractiveness than handsomeness.

Since his mother's death, he had lived in rooms in Albany Street during his brief sojourns in England. So Sarah had seen more of him during the last two years than since her childhood.

He was not one of that group of ardent young men who clamoured for her favours. Socially, she saw little of him. He professed to dislike the theatre or dancing or boating. He was still a quiet, serious man with a predilection for books and almost an inborn withdrawal from women. Sarah had decided that he was a natural celibate until she saw him one evening at Covent Garden with a raven-haired, foreign-looking beauty. The woman's gestures were possessive and demanding: Martin was attentive and seemed to show little interest in the opera.

Sarah's spirits had sunk to a very low ebb and none of the gaiety which followed the visit to the theatre could rouse her to her former vivacity. She had never seen him with that woman or any other since that evening and she did not like to ask him about her even in a teasing vein.

She did not know when she had first realized that she loved Martin. Was it at Thomas' wedding when she had thought of his possible marriage one day and known a fierce, disturbing jealousy? Or had it come gradually during the last two years when he had frequently impressed her with his quiet strength of character, his fine qualities, his serious and worthwhile outlook and his unfailing kindness and courtesy? He contrasted favourably with the men she knew who were frivolous and light-hearted and irresponsible. But Martin, of course, was not a youth. He was thirty-five, a responsible and considerate man.

She was dreading the arrival at the house when he would probably bid her farewell and drive away. She tried to think of some excuse to ask him into the house, to detain him for a little longer. They were so seldom alone and never did he treat her as anything but a young sister.

"Am I boring you?" he asked abruptly as she made some absent reply to his discussion on the latest development in politics. She was usually so keen-witted, so shrewd, so intelligent — and he had a great respect for her knowledgeable opinion on current affairs.

She was startled. "Of course not. Why?"

He smiled. "Because you haven't heard a word, Sarah. Where are your thoughts . . . with that reckless young devil, Fitzgerald?"

She threw him a quizzical glance. "Alan? I should say not! Why should you think so, anyway?"

"Well . . . he hinted that he hoped to announce his engagement to you in the near future," he admitted, a little reluctantly.

She was swiftly annoyed. "He's a little too confident! He knows very well that I won't marry him! Surely you didn't believe him?"

He shook his head, his eyes twinkling. "No, I didn't. I can't see the beautiful Miss Fallow married to an extravagant and careless young rake."

"I shall marry a much older man . . . if I marry," she told him firmly.

He glanced at her quickly. "Of course you'll marry. Probably one of those ardent young swains who dog your footsteps. You're much too young to discard the possibility of marriage, my dear."

She flushed a little and toyed with her gloves. "Martin . . . aren't you ever going to get married?" she asked impulsively. She glanced at him almost shyly and saw his face close against her question, noted the abrupt darkening of his eyes and the tightening of his mouth. "Am I tactless?" she went on slowly, hesitantly. "I don't mean to pry, Martin — but you'd make such a wonderful husband for some woman."

"You're so sure of that?" he asked bitterly and a nerve jumped at the corner of his mouth.

He drew up outside the house at that moment and leaned over to open the car door.

"Will you come in for a few minutes?" she asked and her eyes held a plea. Big blue eyes that were lustrous in their beauty and few men could resist their appeal.

Martin gazed down at his lovely

166

cousin and suddenly felt that this life had been wasted, empty, meaningless. Where had he taken the wrong path? Wilful though Sarah might be, wayward and reckless and adamant where her wishes were concerned, often rashly sympathetic to the lesser fortunate, embarrassingly outspoken . . . yet with all these things, an inner goodness shone from her eyes and he knew that an indomitable spirit and a rare purity burned within her breast. He felt suddenly unclean, as though he dare not associate with her for fear of tainting her purity, yet his actions in the past had been swayed by an impulse of good intent. The fact that he had later denied them and kept them secret made him a deceiver — and before the honesty in Sarah's eyes, he was ill at ease.

He shook his head. "Sorry . . . but I've an appointment," he lied.

She was too firmly in control of her emotions to allow her lip to quiver with disappointment and she gave no sign of the hurt that he should lie to her . . . for he was a poor liar and his expression of contrition was a thin covering for his deceit.

Her eyes continued to smile at him as she said lightly: "Then perhaps we'll meet at the Claremont party next week. You've been invited, of course."

He paused briefly. "Yes . . . but I don't think I shall go, Sarah. I've had a little experience of their parties." His glance was rueful. "I'm invariably bored." This was no lie for social functions were not his measure of enjoyment.

She exerted a gentle pressure on his arm. "Do come — and I promise you an evening free from boredom."

He laughed. "I wouldn't reach your side for the many admirers who swarm about you — and you won't notice my absence, my dear."

She stepped on to the pavement and turned with a light smile that did not betray the ache in her heart or the disappointment she felt that she could not persuade him to attend the party.

"Then I shall see you one of these days," she said carelessly. "Thanks for the lift, Martin. 'Bye." And she turned away, searching in her bag for the door key . . .

Nevertheless, Martin decided to accept the invitation — and scarcely knew what prompted him to change his mind. He arrived before Sarah and found himself talking to a fat and shapeless dowager who was a distant relative of his mother's.

Sarah made a grand entrance. Pausing briefly in the doorway of the big room, she was a figure to draw the eyes and attention of all and swift murmurs of appreciation and question ran round the room. Her golden hair was bound smoothly about her head and secured with an ornament of deepest jet. Her slim body was encased in a gown of black and silver. Her lovely complexion and brilliant blue eyes and enchanting smile brought a ripple of admiring comment.

Martin's words faded into silence as

169

he stared at his cousin. The old lady by his side looked at him shrewdly with her piercing black eyes. She observed the almost desperate look in his eyes, the instinctive half-movement towards the door, the sudden catch of his breath.

She tapped him sharply on the arm. "She's a beauty now — but one day she'll be fat and ugly like me, boy," she told him with a cackle of laughter. "Stake your claim to the minx if you want her — or you'll find it impossible once the vultures have made their excuses and gravitated towards her. Go, Martin boy . . . I won't keep you — anyone can see how you feel about the girl."

Martin felt a dull flush surge to his cheeks. He told himself not to be a fool . . . that he was not an inexperienced youth but a man in full control of his emotions. It was ridiculous to tremble with swift desire and yearn to rush across the room to Sarah . . . the girl he had always thought of as a sister.

But an impish devil mocked him. A

sister . . . had he really thought of her in that way during the last two years when it had been an effort not to seek her company, when he had forced himself to avoid social functions where they must meet, when he had tried to evict all tumultuous thought and feelings out of his brain and heart.

Before then . . . when he was abroad and they had exchanged letters . . . How well he had come to know Sarah through her quaint, impulsive and cool little letters — the times when he had sensed that she swiftly and sternly repressed sentiment from the penned words had caused tenderness to surge. He felt that he must have loved her from that first day when his father had brought her to The Meads . . . he had been captivated by her infant beauty, the broad, sweet and entirely spontaneous smile, the eager and yet natural acceptance of his admiration and instant affection. He had watched her grow from infancy to childhood, from childhood to adolescence — and then to maturity and always love for his 'golden girl' had lived in his heart, firmly suppressed because he considered that he had no right to love her, tormenting him considerably during the last two years when he had spent more time in England than before.

Remaining by the old lady's side, he forced a smile and a light quip fell smoothly from his tongue. But he knew that she was not deceived. Firmly, he kept his gaze away from Sarah — but within a few minutes he felt a gentle hand on his arm and turned to look into her face.

"So you came, Martin."

He smiled. Her remark scarcely warranted a reply but he murmured some polite affirmative. Then he introduced her to his relative and he noticed that she returned the old lady's piercing look without a swerve of her honest eyes or a flinch of her lovely face.

As soon as courtesy allowed, she

turned back to her cousin. Music began to fill the room and she smiled graciously at him. He recognized her smile as a coquettish invitation and he could not resist her obvious desire to dance.

She was light as a feather in his arms and every movement was smooth and graceful. She was gay, vivacious and talkative, her cheeks flushed prettily and her eyes very bright. Her nearness was disturbing and he found it difficult to concentrate on his steps.

She kept her promise and he found the evening both amusing and diverting. Skilfully she warded off most of her admirers: occasionally she danced with one of them, explaining to Martin in a whispered aside that she dare not offend them beyond recall. He found her company and conversation stimulating. By the end of the evening, he was even more bound by the call of his heart and by his desire for her.

He asked if he could take her home. She threw him a laughing glance. "My dear Martin . . . do you want to fight half of male London? I always make a point of leaving parties alone . . . Cathryn calls for me in a taxi so that I have company."

"Then may I see you tomorrow?"

She was serious for a brief moment. Then she gave him her hand and pressed his fingers affectionately. "Of course. Come in the morning . . . I shall love to see you. In any case, I want you to see Daniel — he thrives amazingly and, I regret to add, grows more like his father every day."

Martin frowned slightly. He had not approved of her action in offering Cathryn Manners and her child a home — and this had been the basis of their only quarrel. Martin had been out-argued for Sarah was obstinately convinced of the rightness of her action. Generously, he had helped in every possible way — and to please her, had stood as godparent to Daniel at his christening, winning her undying gratitude.

The frown faded and he assured her that he would be delighted to see his little godson. He added abruptly: "You know, Sarah, you're a very kind person. Not many people would bother about a servant and her illegitimate child."

"George Marchmont is the one who should bother," she said angrily. "It was the devil's own job to get him to give Cathryn ten pounds a month. As he won't do anything else for her then I must do it for him. I'm afraid I have a very low opinion of George these days — and I'm very disappointed in Louise."

He said shrewdly: "Perhaps she guessed the truth. One can hardly expect her to give the girl kindness and sympathy or even help when George was the cause of it all."

"Poor Cathryn."

"Poor Louise," he amended swiftly. "She is the one to be pitied, you know. Cathryn is well provided for and her future is assured while she stays with you. Louise's happiness was short-lived and I don't suppose she welcomes the future with open arms."

Sarah sighed. "I wish there were some way to force him to behave better. I used to like him. I didn't know him well but at least I believed that he loved Louise and would never do anything to hurt her. However," she added with no trace of sentiment, "Louise has been very foolish and one can almost sympathize with George — he's not her husband but merely the father of her children, I'm afraid."

With this remark, she said goodnight to him, made her farewells to the Claremonts and left to find Cathryn waiting for her with the taxi . . .

When Martin called the following morning, he found Sarah in the sitting-room with Daniel in her arms. She turned with an eager smile. He came forward and kissed her cheek and then gave his strong, slender finger to the boy to grip.

"Well, how is Daniel today?"

She looked at him with faint anxiety.

"Do you think it was a suitable name?"

He smiled. "You chose it — and although you've never told me why, I think I can give a good guess."

She smiled mischievously. "Well?"

"'Dare to be a Daniel'," he quoted, "and no doubt the poor child will have to stand alone all his life."

"That's what I'm afraid of," she admitted. "Cathryn is so independent and won't let me help any more than I have done. She cares for Daniel herself. She doesn't like it if I buy clothes or toys for him. She doesn't like me to devote too much time to him. She argues that he's the son of a servant and she doesn't want him to grow up in the atmosphere of wealth and luxury."

He said grimly: "He's also the son of a wealthy man descended from a noble family."

The door opened and Cathryn Manners came into the room. She was an attractive young woman with rich brown hair, velvety brown eyes and naturally red lips. Often, studying her physical attraction — the slim waist, the high breasts, the narrow hips and flanks, the long, slender legs — Martin could understand why George Marchmont had been tempted.

She nodded courteously to Martin and came forward to take her son from Sarah's arms. "It's time for his feed, Miss Fallow."

"He's looking very well," Martin said, smiling. "He's going to be a handsome child."

She did not look at him. Cathryn seldom looked at any man. "I hope not, sir," she replied. "Good looks are the instrument of the devil." And with this gloomy remark she went from the room.

Martin stared at Sarah and then laughed aloud. "Where did she get that from?" he demanded.

Sarah smiled. "Cathryn has recently taken her religion very seriously. She feels the burden of her sin lies heavily on her shoulders, you know."

"Silly woman," he said indulgently.

He sat in a deep armchair, crossed one leg over the other and regarded his cousin thoughtfully. Her dress of light green was very attractive. He preferred to see her golden hair coiled neatly on the nape of her neck. He said impulsively: "What a lovely creature you are, Sarah!"

She coloured faintly at the compliment. "Will you have some coffee, Martin?"

He held out his hand. "Come here, my dear one. Don't offer me coffee — I want to talk to you very seriously."

Obediently, a little bewildered, she went to him and placed her hand trustingly within the firm clasp. He drew her on to his knees.

"Please . . . Martin!" she exclaimed, startled.

"You're not afraid of me?" he asked in surprise. "I won't hurt you, Sarah." His touch was gentle, his dark eyes reassuringly warm and his voice held a note of pain that she should struggle against him.

Abruptly she relaxed and laid her

head on his shoulder. He held her close, not tightly but neither loosely and his embrace was strangely comforting. Sarah felt secure and oddly happy yet deep within her heart she felt that he had come to tell her something disturbing, something which did not promise happiness.

"Well?" she pressed. His words might be painful or unpleasant but she was not afraid to face up to things and she very much wanted to know the reason for his tender yet anxious words.

"Sarah, I've no right to say what's in my heart — but I must tell you that I love you. I believe that you love me a little — not just in a sisterly way — but in the way a woman loves a man. I love you dearly. My life would be empty without you in it somewhere. I wish I could ask you to marry me . . . but that isn't possible."

"Martin! You don't disapprove of marriage between cousins, surely?" she exclaimed, sitting upright.

He shook his head. "That isn't the

reason." He searched her blue, anxious eyes. "You believe that I love you — with all my heart?"

She sighed. "Yes, I do."

"And you care for me a little?"

She touched his cheek with her lips, shyly, softly, with all the tenderness that her heart held for him. "More than a little, Martin. I've always loved you, I think."

He stifled a groan . . . but not quickly enough. She scanned his face rapidly. He touched her cheek with his long, slender fingers. "My dear — I said I had no right to mention my love. Certainly I haven't the right to hold you, to know your nearness, to ask if you love me."

"Why not?" Her voice was low, stifled, fraught with the hint of tears. But he knew she would not cry: Sarah was too courageous, too proud and too considerate. She could take even a death-blow without flinching — and certainly he must deal their love a death-blow.

181

"Because, Sarah, I'm a married man."

She caught her breath. "No! You can't be! How can you be married? When? To whom? Why don't we know about it?"

He laid a finger against her lips. "So many questions. I'll try to explain. I married an Italian girl five years ago. She's the daughter of Count Auguste de Lucco. I was madly infatuated and insisted on marrying her but within six months I knew I'd made a mistake. I didn't love her — it was impossible that I could ever love her. We are worlds apart."

"Then you don't . . . live together?" she asked quietly.

"She's living in my house in Vienna. She's a Catholic, of course — and divorce is out of the question. I'm tied to Giana for life . . . and yet I love you."

"Why didn't you tell me before?" she demanded passionately.

"I didn't tell anyone. I wasn't

particularly proud of having made a fool of myself."

Sarah fell silent. She was quiet for a long time. He wisely said no more: made no move to kiss her; kept her on his knee with his arm lightly about her waist. She sat with downcast eyes and a stony expression and her thoughts were tumultuous and distressed.

At last he said gently: "You're angry with me, Sarah."

She looked up then. "Anger is rather futile," she said coolly. "I'm hurt and disappointed, yes . . . but not angry. I can understand and sympathize with you. I'm also very sorry for your wife."

Dull colour stormed to his cheeks. "Don't waste your pity, my dear! Giana is utterly immoral, spoilt and extravagant and she cares nothing for me. She married me partly because she wanted a wealthy husband, partly because she imagined that marriage to an Englishman would give her a certain position. Her father encouraged the match . . . and, as I've told you, I was madly infatuated. Since I married Giana, she has had a dozen lovers — and flaunts them in my face whenever I visit her which I feel compelled to do every few months. No, my dearest, don't waste your pity," he added, more quietly.

She put her arm about his neck and drew him to her. With infinite gentleness and love, she laid her mouth on his and kissed him. He sighed and drew her closer. Then she moved restlessly and freed herself from his arms.

"No, Martin . . . " She stood up and began to pace the room, hands clasped before her, eyes thoughtful. "I've always hoped to marry you one day, Martin," she said quietly, without embarrassment, without shyness.

"Oh, darling . . . " He leaped to his feet and came towards her, hands outstretched.

"No!" She turned on him with the first sign of anger. "You must never kiss me again — never! As a married man, you owe your wife a certain loyalty — whether or not you love her! I won't encourage you to behave like a George Marchmont — and I suppose I'm not really as unconventional as I thought," she added more quietly.

He paused in his tracks and his eyes were dark with pain. "That isn't a very nice thing to say to me. You're judging me too harshly."

She ignored him. "We can never be married — that's obvious," she said bitterly.

"What are we going to do?" There was a note of desperation in his voice. At that moment, every nerve in his body was alive with the need of her, every pulse drummed out his love for her.

Her expression was strangely matter of fact but she was pale and her eyes seemed inexpressibly weary. "You're going to Vienna, dear Martin. You're going back to your wife to try to make a success of your marriage. Let everyone know that you're married and bring your wife to England to be made known to your family and friends. You haven't been fair or kind — and I didn't think you were capable of behaving so badly to anyone."

He stared his astonishment. "You don't know what you are suggesting, Sarah! You really want me to return to that . . . wanton and deny my love for you? Can a man deny the beat of his heart, the flow of blood in his veins, his need for meat and drink? Sarah, my darling!"

"It's going to be hard . . . but it's what I want you to do," she said with quiet decision.

"Yet you claim to love me?"

She turned on him fiercely. "I do love you. It's breaking my heart . . . can't you see that? But I won't snatch at happiness while that poor woman doesn't have affection, respect or even consideration from you. What do you want from me, Martin? You can't marry me . . . what else did you think to offer?" Her tone was scornful.

He crossed the room forcefully and took her into his arms, holding her close. Her eyes were frank and fearless as she met his gaze.

"I've nothing to offer you, my dear," he said quietly, gently. "But I wanted you to know that I love you — that I shall go on loving you for the rest of my life. I hoped that I might have a little of your love. I wanted you to know that I can't marry you but that nothing can prevent me from loving you. I wanted just once to have my arms about you — like this," and his embrace tightened. "I wanted just once to press my lips to yours — like this," and he sought her mouth hungrily and yet with the sweet, gentle tenderness born of love.

Sarah clung to him, responding to that kiss with all the passionate ardour of her youthful heart. When they finally broke away, Martin was trembling and he turned away to fight for his self-control.

She laid a hand on his arm. "Oh,

I do understand!" she cried. "I know how hard it is for you . . . it is for me, my darling. But we must be sane and sensible and reasonable — and we mustn't ever be together like this again or speak of our feelings to each other."

He ran his hands through his dark hair until it stood in a crest over his head. He was white and strained and unhappy. He did not know what he had hoped for — but he had not expected her to be so firm, so resolute. He had not expected this bleak and utter hopelessness for the future — a vision of painful emptiness and longing and despair — an eternal ache in his heart and loins for the woman he loved.

"Sarah — I'd do anything for you," he said quietly. "Except live with Giana again. You must see how impossible that is — loving you as I do. It would be absolute hell! Please try to believe that she doesn't want me, Sarah. She hates me — certainly she doesn't want to share my life. She hates England

and the English people. She came to London not so long ago and naturally demanded my escort. She was filled with contempt for the city and countryside and she mocked and obviously despised my friends and everyone she met."

Memory flooded Sarah. "Did you take her to Covent Garden, Martin?"

He was puzzled but he replied readily enough: "Yes. She didn't think very highly of our operatic singers or the production. Why?"

"I was there," she said slowly. "I saw you."

"I sat back so I shouldn't be seen too clearly," he told her. "Giana, of course, loving attention and admiration, commandeered the front of the box." He smiled a little grimly. "Well, my dear, you've seen my wife — do you still pity her?"

"She's very beautiful." Honesty compelled the words.

He laughed bitterly. "On the surface, yes. Didn't Cathryn say that good looks are the instrument of the devil? It's true enough where Giana is concerned. She's beautiful but she has an ugly nature, an evil nature." His face held a shadow of hatred and loathing.

"Martin! Don't look so malignant! How much you hate and despise her! I can't make you go back to her, of course — that's your business. But I won't cheapen myself or our love by letting you make love to me again," she said decisively. "We must go on as we have always done. Good friends — casual meetings — formal courtesy in public — but never, never any display of affection on either side. Promise me, Martin — you must promise!" She did not plead: she commanded. He knew that her determined will would have its way and he could think of nothing that would change her mind.

"Do you think that love is so sinful, Sarah?" he asked sadly. She gave him a swift, penetrating, reproachful glance from her beautiful eyes and he wished the words unspoken. He said hastily:

"Oh, I promise — if it's what you want — but I don't understand you. Surely we're entitled to a little happiness in this life?"

"Not at someone else's expense," she protested.

He gave a little shrug. "As if Giana would care!"

"But I would."

He took her hands and looked down at her with his heart in his eyes. "If you were any other woman, Sarah, I'd ask you to live with me as my wife. No one but you in this country knows that I'm married. But you wouldn't be happy, would you? For you, it's marriage or nothing, whatever the circumstances." He tried to keep bitterness, disappointment, reproach from his voice but he knew that he was not successful.

"You think I'm being hard and cruel, Martin," she told him quietly.

He nodded. "A little."

"I love you too much, perhaps." She smiled faintly. "If I didn't love you so

191

much, Martin, I would live with you — but that kind of loving isn't for either of us, my dear. It has to be marriage or nothing, you see."

When he had gone, raising her hands to his lips with such passionate humility that her eyes welled with tears, she sank into a chair and buried her face in her hands.

She had been honest with him and with herself. She loved him as she could never love any other man — but their love was too precious for them to take their happiness lightly in each other's arms. Though her body might ache with desire for him, though her heart might seem to burst with love for him, she could not be other than what she was — and Martin was too essentially good, too essentially honest to find lasting happiness in an illegal liaison . . .

Sarah paused on the steps to wave a careless hand to Alan Fitzgerald. She had been to Henley with him that afternoon for he was still attentive, still hopeful, despite the many refusals she had given him and despite the fact that she treated him exactly the same as every one of her many men-friends.

Standish — much older and stooping painfully — greeted her and Sarah smiled at him as she walked across the hall. She opened the door of the sitting-room and went in, humming softly, vaguely aware that the old man was muttering something indistinct in the background.

She paused at the sight of a young woman with her back to the door, standing by the window. There was something familiar about that proud, dark head: the slim shoulders and arrogant bearing struck a note of recognition. Then the woman turned slowly and their eyes met across the room.

Ann was the first to speak. "Well, Sarah — do you mean to throw me out of the house or are you more human and understanding than most?"

Sarah moved towards her, hands

outstretched, her warmly compassionate heart touched by the sadness in her sister's eyes and the wan, drawn features.

"Ann ... it's been such a long time," she said gently, drawing her towards a long couch. "Do sit down and let me have a good look at you."

Ann smiled crookedly. "Looking for signs of dissipation? I came here from Louise's house — we were brought up together, after all, and I felt sure that some spark of her affection for me must linger." She bit her lip, paused and went on: "She refused to see me and sent me a brief message requesting that I would not call again — that she thought it inadvisable for me to meet her children at any time."

Sarah caught her breath. Hastily, trying to excuse Louise's action, she said: "She's awfully unhappy, Ann. George is a most unsatisfactory husband ... you must try to make allowances. She's been ill, too, ever since she had her last baby."

"Another one?"

"A little boy . . . Hugh. He's nearly a year old now." She dismissed the subject. "How is Freddie? How long have you been in London? Do tell me all your news, Ann."

Ann gestured wearily. "I should have written to you . . . warned you that I was coming back. I was fairly certain of Louise's reception but I meant to ask you if I could stay here for a while . . . until I make other arrangements. Blood is thicker than water, Sarah — you must help me . . . there isn't anyone else who will." There was a hint of bitter desperation in her voice.

Sarah said practically: "Before we talk, you must have some coffee — you look pale and your hands are like ice." She rose and rang the bell. As they waited, she studiously avoided any mention of Ann's affairs. Instead, she talked of Thomas and his success in Italy. Ann remarked listlessly that she had seen him only a few months ago: she and Freddie had stayed in Rome for a week. They had dined at the villa and Mariana had made them very welcome: the little girl was both pretty and well-mannered.

Coffee came and Sarah poured the hot, aromatic liquid into the delicate cups. Ann watched her and then she said abruptly: "How old are you — twenty-two? You don't seem interested in marriage — you must be the only sensible member of the family." Again that bitter note.

Sarah coloured swiftly. She handed the coffee to her sister and said as lightly as she could: "Oh, I'll marry when the right man comes along. So far he's managed to elude me."

Ann stirred the coffee, leaning back against the couch with obvious gratitude for its comfort. She said slowly: "I've been a fool, Sarah — a complete and utter fool. Do you know that?"

Sarah did not look at her. "If you'd like to talk about it . . . "

"Like to talk about it? My dear, I'm dying to talk to someone." She laughed a little harshly. "Thomas told me about the girl who lives with you . . . didn't she have a child by George? I realized that you must be a kind and compassionate woman — and I wondered if you might be willing to help me. That's why I came here. You may not wish to help me, of course — I may not have the same appeal as an unmarried mother. After all, I'm only to blame for my unhappiness — but I gather that the girl was an unfortunate innocent."

"Tell me how I can help you," Sarah said decisively.

Ann stared. "You mean that, don't you . . . yet I haven't told you the full story yet."

"It doesn't matter, Ann. If you don't want to tell me, I shall understand — and you're welcome here as long as you wish to stay. If there's anything I can do, please ask me." Sarah smiled gently at her sister. What had happened to the gay, vivacious and reckless Ann? She had been a lovely woman — now she was haggard and drawn, looking ill, her body painfully thin and her hair neglected and lank. Sarah found it hard to believe that any amount of unhappiness could have brought Ann to such a state of mind that her appearance no longer counted. She had always been brave — with the courage born of indifference rather than anything else. Certainly it did not seem feasible that folly and sin could break her indomitable spirit.

Ann was silent for a while. Then she began: "Do you remember my contempt of convention? I told you once that conventions were made for fools . . . like rules. Well, I defied convention when I ran away with Freddie. I expect you condemned me . . . everyone else did. But they didn't consider my point of view, you know. I married Vince when I was barely eighteen and he was twenty years older. I was flattered that he wanted to marry me . . . a mere girl with little money and more love for the country than for the whirl of society. He was wealthy and his estates were beautiful and covered a great deal of acres. He promised me so many things. But when we were married, I realized that he didn't love me at all . . . he'd married me with the same cool calculation that he'd feel if he bought an old and valuable antique. I was beautiful — and he wanted to own me." She broke off to cough painfully.

Sarah refilled her cup. She did not comment on Ann's story so far — and she felt that Ann appreciated her silence.

The bout of coughing over, Ann smiled an apology — and with that smile came a trace of the lovely girl she had been and Sarah could understand why Vincent Riley with his passion for beauty and his rare collection of beautiful things had wanted to possess the exquisite creature that Ann had been at eighteen.

"Freddie was handsome — and he was young which was a very important reason for falling in love with him. He was young and gay and attentive. He had a very persuasive tongue. He assured me that he loved me . . . I think he did for a while." Her mouth twisted suddenly with the pain of memory. "So I went away with him — and it was wonderful: fun, unconventional, exciting and reckless. Freddie swore he'd be faithful to me . . . I wrote and begged Vince to divorce me so we could be married but he didn't reply. Freddie said it didn't matter — he'd never want any woman but me, anyway. So I was happy enough." She sipped the fresh, hot coffee. A little colour was returning to her cheeks: her lips did not look so pinched. Sarah noticed that her hands shook slightly so that her cup rattled in its saucer. She was silent for a long time and Sarah waited patiently. Glancing at her sister, she saw that two big tears had welled in her dark eyes and with bated breath she watched them spill over and trickle slowly down her cheeks.

Sarah's heart was caught in a grip of

painful pity. Ann had never been the type to seek refuge in tears. As a baby, her only tears had been with temper. A disappointment, a sharp word, a slap — throughout infancy, childhood and adolescence she had merely tossed her head and laughed mockingly. If she cried later, then it was in secret and without witnesses.

Ann turned her head and brushed her hand across her eyes. Pulling herself together, she went on: "I found I was going to have a baby. We were in Berlin . . . Freddie had lots of friends there. I wrote to Vince again and begged him for a divorce — but he didn't reply. When I began to get obviously pregnant, Freddie began to go out alone . . . until he was scarcely ever with me. The day before my daughter was born I discovered that he was having an affair with an Italian girl." Her voice was flat and toneless, inexpressibly weary. "She was pretty notorious . . . everyone called her the *de Lucco*. Her name was Giana, I think." She did not notice Sarah's start of dismay. "Freddie and I quarrelled and he begged me to forgive him. He vowed he loved me — that it would never happen again — that he'd look after me and the child. Two months ago, we left Berlin for Vienna . . . Freddie said he was tired of Berlin. I soon discovered that he was meeting the *de Lucco* again and that she was his mistress and when I found out that her home was in Vienna I understood Freddie's sudden boredom with Berlin."

Sarah spoke for the first time. "Your child?"

"Frances? I brought her with me, of course. I've left her at my hotel with one of the maids . . . I wanted to find out if you were willing to help me before bringing her here."

"Poor little girl!" She wanted to ask so many questions but she restrained them and merely said quietly: "So you walked out on Freddie?"

Ann looked down at her hands.

She twisted the handkerchief which Sarah had tactfully slipped into her lap between her fingers, pulling and tearing and twisting. Suddenly there was a rending noise and she looked down at the two pieces of cambric. Then she burst into laughter — loud and mocking and hysterical. She laughed for long minutes while Sarah tried to hush her without success. At last, Sarah reluctantly slapped her face — and Ann dissolved into silence, burying her face in her hands.

She looked up at last. "I'm sorry . . . I'm tired and worried." Her eyes were strained. "Can I trust you?" she asked. "Really trust you?"

Sarah drew her close and put her arms about the thin shoulders. "Of course you can. I only want to help you."

"No one can help me," she returned dully. "I realize that very well. I'm to blame for everything . . . I hurt Vince and left him without a thought for his feelings . . . I was a married woman but I encouraged Freddie to love me and take me away . . . I have a child who has no right to Vince's name and cannot take Freddie's name."

"Hush, darling, it's over now," Sarah soothed. "You can stay here until you are well and happy again . . . just like the Ann we used to know. Then perhaps you could see Vincent — talk things over. He might take you back . . . "

"You don't understand!" Her voice was harsh. "I can't live with anyone again. I've no right to ask for your help. Freddie is dead, you see."

Sarah stared at her. "Dead?"

Ann nodded. "Yes . . . I killed him." She said the words flatly and unemotionally. Sarah instinctively recoiled and then, realizing how much her sister needed help and comfort, she clasped her even tighter and gently stroked the dark, unruly hair. "I don't even feel anything," Ann said and now her voice was pitiful. "I know I should . . . I loved him so much, Sarah. He was my world. I couldn't bear to let that woman have him — or any other woman. So I had to kill him. I bought a gun and followed him when he went out — and then I shot them both. Freddie, because I loved him too much and he let me down — that woman because I hated her for what she had done to me and so many other women!"

Sarah released her and leaped to her feet, pacing the room, her hands to her face, trying to think coolly. She could hardly believe the story . . . yet it had the absolute ring of truth. Ann had calmly killed Freddie and his mistress in Vienna . . . no wonder she looked so ill and distraught. She was sick in mind and body. Sarah could not imagine how Ann had managed to leave Vienna without being checked.

She turned sharply. "The police?"

Ann shrugged. "I killed Freddie — and then stood by his body to shoot the woman. She screamed and screamed . . . it was horrible!" She gave a faint shudder. "The police think it was murder followed by Freddie's suicide. The *de Lucco* had a reputation and no one was surprised that she had been killed by one of her lovers. No one suspected me . . . I was prostrate with grief and full of concern for my baby whenever the police tried to question me. They were kind and understanding . . . they believed Freddie was my husband and naturally thought I'd been distressed enough without questions to embarrass me."

"Ann . . . Ann! Do you realize what you've done?" Sarah asked helplessly.

"Of course I do. I know it was wrong but what else could I do? Stand back and let that woman have Freddie? Or let Freddie think I didn't know — and put up with a succession of such affairs for the rest of my life? How long do you think he would have stayed with me, anyway — he was already tired of me. He was worthless and immoral — but I do believe he loved me for a little while."

The last words were torn from her

and Sarah realized that this thought was all that had sustained her while she nursed her terrible secret and the knowledge of her sin against society and her own conscience.

She took Ann's hands and exerted a firm, reassuring pressure. "Don't worry . . . I'll help you, Ann. But it's too much for me alone. Trust me, darling. I must talk this over with Martin — he'll be able to advise us both. You can trust him implicitly, I promise. Until I can talk to him, I suggest you go to bed and stay there . . . I'll tell Mrs. Standish to prepare a room for you. You need plenty of rest and plenty of sleep, darling."

"Peace of mind would be more welcome," Ann said unhappily.

Sarah was surprised that she did not protest against her suggestion of enlisting Martin's assistance. But perhaps she was beyond resisting . . . she was a sick woman and worry filled her thoughts to the exclusion of all else.

Sarah quickly took charge. Ann was

soon ensconced in one of the bedrooms
and a maid sent to the hotel to bring
Frances to the house. The child was
small and thin and pale. Her hair was
as dark as Ann's but her eyes were the
vivid blue of Sarah's own.

When she could relax and think over
Ann's story, Sarah battled with the
emotions and hopes of her heart. The
name could not be mere coincidence.
Giana *de Lucco*! It could only be
Martin's wife — and in the most
terrible way possible, Martin's freedom
was assured. Sarah allowed herself to
dwell briefly on the possibility that she
and Martin could take their happiness
at last . . . due to the hand of her own
sister!

Martin was out of London and
Sarah was dismayed. It was unlike
him to leave the city without letting
her know. He probably had his reasons
for his unexpected absence but it was
annoying that he should be away just
when she needed him.

Ann was behaving very strangely. She

refused to see her child and would not have anything to do with her. She screamed at the servants and sent them from her room. She accused Sarah of sending them to spy on her and her half-hooded eyes gleamed with distrust and fear.

Sarah was anxious, wondering if she should send for a doctor, telephoning Martin's flat again and again in vain, trying to assure Ann that she was in safe hands and that no one intended to call in the police . . .

On the second night in the house, when all was still and quiet, Ann rose and dressed herself carefully, neatly fastening her dark hair with more care than she had given it for some time. Then she silently crept into the room where her daughter was sleeping.

For a long time, Ann looked down at Frances, sleeping so innocently . . . the child born of her reckless love for Freddie. A child born without a name. The child of an immoral rogue and a murderess.

With infinite pity and tenderness, Ann pressed her lips to that peaceful brow. She brushed back a dark strand of the child's hair . . . then with tears running down her cheeks but a firm determination burning in her breast, she took up a cushion and placed it over the child's face. She held it there for what seemed an eternity, convinced that she was doing the only possible thing. There was bad blood in the child and her future would be very dark if she lived.

Then she threw down the cushion and hurried out of the room. Leaving the house, she hailed a passing taxi, not caring that she received an odd and curious glance from the cabbie. She directed him to the Embankment. Once there, she gave him the contents of her purse, shrugged aside his exclamation of protest and turned away.

The Embankment was deserted. Slowly, Ann wandered to the parapet and looked down at the swirling eddy of dark water. She had brought disgrace on the family. She had no future, having forfeited all right to happiness or peace of mind. It seemed that there was nothing for her to live for now . . .

She looked down into the murky river, cool and collected and unafraid. She heard the deliberate, even step of a passing constable and quickly drew into the shadows of Cleopatra's Needle. She waited with pounding heart while he paused a few yards away. He was humming a gay little tune and bitterness engulfed her. She willed him to walk on — and at last heard again the steady pacing along the dark and lonely pavement.

Ann walked to the head of the steps. Slowly she walked down to the river. She paused for a brief moment as the water lapped about her feet . . . then she walked on without further hesitation. She did not resist the cool, welcoming embrace of the water — and it rose to embrace her like an old friend . . . caressed her slim hips, hugged her neat waist, eagerly kissed breast and shoulders, caught the strands of her face. This was the only way, the easy way — and for the first time in her life, Ann Fallow surrendered to cowardice.

Her dark hair loosened from its pins under the tug and swirl of the waters, hungry for its new companion, and then it floated back on the surface of the water . . .

Her body was found the next morning.

Sarah went to Ann's room and found it empty, her clothes gone. The maid in charge of Frances came rushing into the room at the sound of her step.

"Such a scare I had last night, ma'am," she said, half-sobbing. "I dreamed that little Miss Frances was in terrible danger . . . it was so vivid that it woke me up . . . terrible it was, ma'am. I saw a dark shadow in the room and I was paralysed with fright. Then I got out of bed and ran to the cot . . . Miss Frances was black in the face and breathing funny-like so I ran for Mr. Standish . . ."

Sarah cut the recital short. "Is the baby all right?"

"Oh yes, ma'am. Mr. Standish told me to keep her warm and give her some hot milk. He sent for the doctor straight away."

Sarah went in search of Standish. Very distressed, he explained the whole thing more lucidly, adding that the little girl had been almost suffocated, according to the doctor."

Sarah pulled at her lip. "But surely . . . was she given a pillow?" she asked angrily. "A baby of that age should never have a pillow!"

His expression was distant. Sarah left him abruptly, fear surging in her heart. Poor Ann! Where had she gone? Back to Vincent Riley — without a baby to explain away which might spoil her hopes of reconciliation? But Ann would not have left the house at night — nor without word to her sister. Where could she be?

She was not long in doubt. About Ann's throat was a locket containing two miniatures, one of herself as a bride and one of Vincent Riley. She had deliberately slipped it about her neck before setting out on her errand . . . an errand from which she never returned.

The police contacted Vincent Riley, took him to the mortuary and asked him if he could identify the dead woman. It was a painful blow to the man to recognise her as the wife he had loved and lost to another man . . .

It was some weeks before Sarah could accept the truth that it was perhaps for the best. Poor Ann might have escaped the consequences of her crime in the legal sense — but would she ever have been able to escape her conscience and the burden of guilt?

Frances quickly recovered from the attempted suffocation. Sarah dealt with the nurse by dismissing her tales of a dark shadow as fanciful imagination and her dream motivated by the whimpers of the baby. For she was determined that the incident should be accepted as merely an accident — although she could only guess at the truth she had little doubt that her sister had intended to kill her child before taking her own life.

She was very anxious to see and talk to Martin but she was denied the opportunity for some weeks. Then he came instantly to the house where Sarah was waiting for him, having heard that he was back in London and cancelling all her engagements so that she would be free to welcome him.

He took her hands and looked down at her with warm compassion in his eyes. "My poor Sarah. You've had a rough time, I hear."

"Ann?" she queried.

He nodded. "Yes, I met a friend at the Club." He grimaced a little ruefully. "Loquacious friends can have their uses."

She released her hands and moved to pour coffee into the delicate little cups. "I'm glad you're home, Martin," she said simply.

"I'm sorry I had to go abroad at a time when you needed me," he said sincerely. "You must have wondered what took me abroad so urgently."

"It was obvious," she told him. "Ann came here, you know — and she told me about Freddie . . . and your wife."

He looked at her quickly. "I see . . . So that's why she did it? My information was that she and Freddie had parted some weeks before . . . that wasn't true, I gather?"

"No . . . they were still living together."

"Poor girl — betrayed by the man she loved, upset by the scandal, a child to provide for and no one to turn to — except you, Sarah."

"And I failed her," she said quietly. "I didn't know what she wanted me to say . . . I couldn't give her the one thing she wanted — and I still don't know what it was!"

His glance was warmly affectionate. "Sarah, I doubt if even Ann knew what she really wanted — and you mustn't blame yourself for her death." He reached out for her hand. "Darling, I'm not being callous — but do you realize that I'm a free man now . . . that we can be married? I'm afraid I can't pretend to mourn Giana. Our marriage was a disastrous mistake and I'm grateful for this unexpected release. Oh, I'm sorry that she's dead — but I can't help being thankful for this wonderful chance of happiness with you, Sarah."

Suddenly Sarah knew that she could never tell even Martin the truth . . . Martin who had always been her confidant, her closest and dearest friend, her dear and loyal love. All her life she must keep the secret of Ann's folly and crime. She could not betray her own sister and it would serve no purpose to confide in Martin.

With despair touching her heart, she knew that she could not marry Martin. She could not take advantage of what Ann had done to find her own happiness. She could not know peace of mind, knowing that she owed her marriage to her sister's hand.

She looked at the man she loved and saw the deeply etched lines of pain and suffering in his dear face — and wondered that she could consider denying him the right to a happiness he had long wanted, could deny herself the joy of belonging to the man she had loved for so long, could deny both of them the fulfilment of hopes and dreams that had been stifled for too many years.

But she had no choice. Marriage with this man was no more possible now than it had ever been.

She deliberately schooled her expression to calm serenity. "Married? But . . . Martin, I don't understand. I'm going to marry Alan . . . Alan Fitzgerald. Didn't you know?" Incredulity, dismay and pain flashed into his eyes. "No . . ." he said slowly. "No, I didn't know, Sarah."

She stilled the sudden anguished cry of her heart against the lie she had spoken, against the agony of lost dreams in his eyes. "I'm sorry, Martin," she said gently.

He rose abruptly, thrusting a hand into his pocket to take out his cigarette case. For some moments, he was silent, occupying himself with lighting a cigarette, his mind and heart a confusion of emotions. He could not believe that she meant to marry another man! He was so sure that she loved him, so sure that she would be as happy and as relieved as himself that now they could be married!

"I see . . . " he said at last. "I should have known that it was too good to be true . . . I should have realized that I'm not meant to know happiness in this life."

"Martin — please!"

He turned on her swiftly. "I made a mistake, that's all! I excel in mistakes, you know. I thought you loved me . . . I thought you knew that I would want to marry you if I ever had my freedom! I'm sorry to have embarrassed

219

you, my dear. Please forget that this conversation took place." He strode to the door.

Sarah knew that one word, one gesture would bring him back . . . back to her arms and her love and the heart which felt that it must surely break. But she was silent. She loved him too much. She could not risk marrying him, knowing what she did, knowing that she would always live with the fear that he would learn the truth, knowing that there could be no peace of mind for either of them once he knew that they owed their happiness to the fact that her sister had murdered his wife and her lover.

He paused by the door and looked at her, sitting so still and calm and serene in her chair — and his lip curled with bitterness. She had changed. She no longer cared for him and she could deal his heart a death-blow without a qualm, without sorrow or regret or compassion. Perhaps later he could find excuses for her, admit that she could not be blamed for believing their love to be hopeless and finding a man who was free to marry her — but for the present he was too hurt and angry and jealous. It did not seem possible that she was planning her marriage to another man . . . not Sarah, his lovely golden girl, the woman who had been so radiant in her love for him a few short months before. Was she then so fickle, so unworthy of his love, so swift to accept the futility of their love for each other that she had found it easy to give her heart to another man?

He said stiffly: "Forgive me . . . I neglected to congratulate you on your engagement. I hope you'll be very happy."

The door closed behind him and Sarah's hand went swiftly to bloodless lips to stifle the sound of his name. He did not understand . . . how could he? In his eyes, she was a shameless flirt, a woman who had encouraged his love, his kisses and caresses, a woman who had led him to believe that she would gladly marry him if it were possible — and now she had thrown his love and his hopes and his plans back in his face as calmly and coolly as though they meant nothing.

Was it the supreme heights of folly to relinquish all that marriage with Martin could mean to them both? Was it madness to allow a scruple, a principle to destroy their happiness?

Perhaps Martin would not understand if he knew the truth. Perhaps he would insist that they need not suffer because of her sister's actions. Perhaps he would refuse to allow such a consideration to weigh with him and sweep her recklessly into marriage. But once they were married . . . would he then glance at her speculatively and remember that her sister had committed murder? Would he be reluctant to bring children into the world, fearing that their blood might be tainted with the mark of Cain? Would he hold her in his arms and remember that he did so freely because her sister had paved the way to their happiness? And could they be happy for long with such grim knowledge always in the back of their minds, the grim spectre of Ann standing between them throughout their life together?

He was too dear, too cherished, too loved — and Sarah knew that it would break her heart completely if their love was tarnished by suspicion and doubt and thoughts of the past.

She had chosen the wisest course, painful though it might be. Martin must believe that she meant to marry Alan . . . and she could go further and fare worse. Alan was kind and considerate, gentle and affectionate. He would probably make a good husband and father . . . and she steeled herself against the instinctive recoil of her heart and body to the thought of marriage and motherhood with the wrong man . . .

4

IT was New Year's Day and the house echoed with the shrill cries and laughter of children.

Sarah Fallow, a little older and more mature, her hair as golden bright as ever and her brilliantly blue eyes warm with pleasure in the day, presided over the party that she had instituted for her nephews and nieces. She loved children and she enjoyed the company and gaiety and zest of the younger members of her family.

Hugh sat on her right. Louise's youngest son, a slender boy, good-looking and a little shy, well-behaved and somewhat dominated by his brother, the self-possessed Lionel who had inherited the imperious, inborn arrogance of the Fallows.

Beside him was Mariana, looking scarcely a day older than when she had married Thomas Fallow. Sarah had always been pleased with the result of her match-making for this was a happy and successful marriage. She was delighted that they had returned to England to live and her first anxiety for her brother's careworn appearance had been relieved with his gradual return to health. The climate of Italy had not, after all, suited him so well as they believed and several bouts of fever had decided them to return to England.

Roma, their thirteen-year-old daughter, was an appealing mixture of her father's artistic sensitivity and her mother's demure serenity. She was a happy, affectionate girl and perhaps the only person who could inspire her cousin Frances to a display of emotion. Frances was an elfin-faced child with dark hair and vivid blue eyes. She had a great love of dramatizing the most ordinary events. Shy and withdrawn, a moody, secretive child, she could be fiery when her swift temper or love of justice was aroused. She seemed to have erected an armour against emotion . . . her only outlet being through drama. She adored acting and it was then that her flamboyant personality was given full rein. Roma was her idol . . . and occasionally she would throw her arms about the older girl or shyly touch her hand — and then Roma would put an arm about her and smile with evident affection. They were in tune with each other in a way that baffled their elders.

When they were together, their favourite pastime was to unearth a large trunk which contained various gowns and kimonos and shawls and lengths of bright materials which Thomas used for his models. Out would come the contents and the two girls would sweep about in contrived costumes with dignified poise and dramatic declarations . . . taking themselves so seriously that Thomas was eventually forced to beg them to take pity on his aching sides. Occasionally he would be inspired by a gesture, a flash of colour, a fleeting expression — and he would cry: "Stand just there . . . no, don't move, Frances — I must capture this . . . " Taking his brushes and palette, he would paint and paint, conscious only of the need to transfer the fleeting beauty to canvas, oblivious to the child's gradually-stiffening limbs. As he worked, he would murmur paeons of praise to the grace of her young body, the swing of long dark hair, the brightness of eyes, the natural fall of a draped shawl. At last, satisfied, he would sigh, throw down his brush, gaze with pleasure at the canvas — and then embrace both girls in a rush of delighted affection.

He declared that Frances was a natural model — she had a gift for posing her slender, rounded limbs, for draping a garment to the best effect, for holding an expression. He told Sarah that she might never be a beauty but that the child possessed a vital fascination, adding that she was a born actress.

Sarah smiled across the table at Lucy Marchmont. The girl was growing up and she would soon leave the finishing school in Switzerland. She was very like her mother with the smooth dark hair, the serene eyes and mobile lips. Sarah often wondered what the girl thought about when she sat silent, her eyes scanning the others, and she often felt that Louise was at a loss where this daughter of hers was concerned. She had plans for her that included a social whirl, a satisfactory marriage and eventual children — but Sarah doubted if Lucy would be so ready to fall in with her mother's plans. A strong will lived behind that air of serenity — and she had never made any secret of her wish to be an artist. Louise had been horrified when Lucy told her that she wanted to live in Paris on the Left Bank: that she wanted to study art and that the thought of being a social butterfly until she married bored her. After many arguments, the girl had been forced to relinquish her dream.

But Louise was not entirely heartless and she had asked Thomas for advice. Now, it was arranged that Lucy should live with Thomas and Mariana in London and work with her uncle in his studio when she left school . . . and compromise by attending the social functions that her mother arranged for her even if she could not promise to enjoy them.

It was fascinating to Sarah to watch these children grow up, to note the family traits, to wonder at what lay in store for them.

It was one of her many regrets that she would never have children of her own. Frances was like her own daughter — but she could not forget that Ann had been guilty of murder and she was constantly anxious that the child's passionate nature might hint at a destiny as grim and desperate as her mother's had been.

Her family often wondered that Sarah had never married. Her beauty, her charm, her sweetness, her many good qualities must surely have brought her the opportunities of marriage in the past. It was still not too late, of course . . . Sarah was only thirty-one, after all . . . but although she had many friends of the opposite sex she did not seem unduly attached to any one of them. No one questioned her. Sarah was not the type of woman to discuss her personal feelings nor did she tolerate the discreet probings of her sister with a good grace. There had been that rumour of an engagement to Alan Fitzgerald a few years before . . . but it had not borne fruit and he had married someone else within a year.

It had never occurred to any of them that Martin might have a very strong claim to her heart. Martin was a lone wolf, a wanderer, a confirmed bachelor, a born celibate, too restless to stay in any one place for long — and Martin was too much a member of the family to be considered in any other light. It had never been any secret that he had been the adopted son of Robert and Elizabeth Fallow but throughout the years the fact had been almost forgotten and he was automatically accepted as a cousin of the same blood. If any suspicion had ever touched their mind that Martin and Sarah were more than fond of each other, they had dismissed the idea laughingly . . . they were cousins and it was inadvisable for cousins to marry even if fate should decree that they fall in love!

The meal over, they wandered into the drawing-room. George relaxed in a deep armchair with a sigh and prepared himself for the boredom of the evening. These family affairs bored him and he would have escaped this party if it had not been for the persuasions of his sons. He thought ruefully of the lively, welcoming atmosphere of the Country Club where he liked to spend his evenings — and of that attractive Carolyn Menshaw who did not seem averse to his attentions despite her youth and the fact that she could take her pick from a dozen men of her own age.

Thomas dispensed drinks and his wife sat down by Sarah on the long settee. Louise, too much mother to ignore her children, supervised the discussion of games and pastimes which brought Frances and Lionel to the verge of a quarrel.

Sarah smiled affectionately at her former governess. "Everything seems to be going smoothly, doesn't it?"

"Your parties are very well planned," Mariana told her lightly.

"Long practice, I expect," she retorted. Her glance rested idly on her sister as she settled the dispute between Frances and Lionel. "Poor Louise never rests, does she? When will she learn that children hate interference? They'll settle their squabbles for themselves — and be the best of friends again within minutes."

"She's scrupulously fair, though," Mariana said quietly.

"Oh, I agree." Sarah stifled a slight

yawn. "I'm tired . . . sorry. I went to a party last night and it went on into the early hours." She chuckled. "I suppose I'm not so young as I used to be . . . these parties are almost too much for me."

"When are you going to settle down, Sarah?"

Sarah raised an eyebrow. "Oh, one day," she said carelessly.

"I don't mean to imply that you're a flirt — but you do rather flit, don't you, darling?"

"From man to man, you mean? I suppose so . . . but it really doesn't mean very much, you know. Life is short — and it could be very empty," she added in a quieter tone.

"When you were a child, I thought you would marry young and have a bevy of infants," Mariana mused idly. "It was always your ambition."

"And end up like Louise? Oh, I suppose that wouldn't have been such a terrible fate," Sarah said with a smile. "But marriage and children are not in my destiny, it seems."

"You're still young," Mariana reminded her.

"Yes . . . " She turned to Thomas almost with gratitude as he came towards them with the drinks on a tray and began to talk to him about the new exhibition of his work that was being arranged. Mariana respected her privacy of thought and did not mention the subject again but she continued to wonder. She had not missed the fleeting pain and longing in Sarah's eyes during that brief interchange — and she wondered if there was more to the young woman's continued spinsterhood than mere preference.

It was nearly two years since Sarah had last seen Martin. She had lost not only his love but his friendship when she lied to him about her intention to marry Alan Fitzgerald. Whenever they did meet, he was cool and distant, scarcely granting her the courtesy of family connection, a far cry from close friend and erstwhile lover that he had been. He had never asked her why she had not married Alan. He had never introduced anything personal into their brief conversations and Sarah had no reason to believe that he might still care for her.

There were many times when she regretted the scruple which had prevented their marriage. There were many times when she wished she could turn back the pages of her life and disregard that scruple and marry Martin and find happiness.

She was not actively unhappy but, as she had half-admitted to Mariana, her life would be empty if it were not for her many friends, the many social activities, the work she did to help the lesser fortunate and the knowledge that Frances needed her to play the role of mother.

Martin had always been a part of her life. Perhaps it had always been more of a background part than anything else for she had seen little of him during her adult years but she had always loved him and known that he was dearer to her than anyone else. She had reconciled herself to the knowledge that she could not marry him while his wife lived . . . and once Giana was dead and the obstacle to their marriage was the knowledge that she had died by Ann's hand, it had not been as difficult to face the futility of her love and hopes as it would have been if she could have looked forward to a life spent with Martin.

But she was a lonely woman — and a woman still very much in love with a man she seldom saw. His coldness hurt her although she could understand that he had been hurt and humiliated by her seeming indifference. He must believe that she had fabricated an engagement rather than admit directly that she did not want to marry him . . . and although this was so far from the truth it was better than having to reveal her real reasons.

She had grown accustomed to heartache, to the unsatisfied longing, to the knowledge that she might never marry and have children of her own. She knew that no other man could ever take Martin's place in her heart — and although there were still men in her life who would gladly marry her, she could not enter into a marriage with a man she could not love.

She knew now that if Martin came to her with the offer of his love and asked her again to marry him that she would do so without hesitation. Better to know a fleeting happiness with him than none at all. Better to take the risk of discovery of her sister's guilt than to live an empty life for many years to come. And perhaps he would never know about Ann. Perhaps she had been foolish to be so afraid, to even concern herself with the fear that he might learn the truth. She was not guilty of Ann's crime. She had done nothing that she should continue to pay the penalty in this way. But it was too late. Martin had put her out of his life with finality . . . and it was unlikely that the chance of becoming his wife would ever come her way again.

She had been wrong and foolish. She knew that now. She had sacrificed not only her own but Martin's happiness — and that was even more important to her. She had sentenced him to a lonely, empty life too — and he had already paid more than enough for the mistake of marrying Giana. Ann had not provided any solution . . . her actions had merely introduced fresh problems — but they had not been insuperable! She had allowed Ann's crime to ruin two more lives . . . as if she had not caused enough distress and suffering.

Sarah knew now that if she could have her life again things would be very different. She would have married Martin with eager joy and made him happy and given him children . . . Instead, she was an unfulfilled, unhappy woman and he was a restless, lonely man.

She did not even have the consolation

and comfort of his friendship . . . and if that could have been salvaged, it would have meant a great deal to her . . .

She dragged her thoughts away from Martin as Thomas said carelessly: "By the way, Sarah . . . how's that protegée of yours getting on? She was an unusual woman . . . always reminded me of a Rembrandt painting."

"Dark and secretive? I don't know where she is these days, Thomas. You knew that I sent her to live at The Meads with the boy . . . I thought the country air would be better for them both. Well, she didn't like it — too quiet and lonely for her, I expect . . . she packed up and left without a word."

"How very odd," Mariana commented. Sarah gave a faint shrug. "For some reason she wanted to sever every tie, I think. Perhaps she thought it was time she fended for herself. But I often wonder where she is — and I miss Daniel very much, of course."

She missed Cathryn Manners, too.

The quiet, reserved woman had made a surprising impact on the house that was scarcely noticed until she went away. It had been no wish of Sarah's that Cathryn and her son should leave London but circumstances had forced her hand.

The strangeness of her household had never occurred to Sarah. She did not welcome criticism from friends or family of the fact that she lived in the big house with no one but Cathryn for a companion and that the boy and her sister's child depended on her kindness and generosity for all the advantages that they enjoyed. Cathryn was a good listener and she attended to the housekeeping duties that irked Sarah. Daniel was a companion for Frances and the two children had been good friends. Cathryn had cared for Frances when she was a baby and Sarah had found no fault with the behaviour and temperament of the little girl.

But as Daniel grew older, he resembled

his father very much. A tall, slim boy with the good breeding of his paternal lineage in his handsome looks, sturdy and graceful body, it was impossible to pretend that he was not George Marchmont's son for the likeness was striking and disconcerting.

It was not difficult to prevent meetings between the boy and Louise and her family for Louise seldom called at the house and the boys were away at school. But Louise arrived unexpectedly one day and met the boy in the hall. He was curious about the strange lady he had never seen: she was filled with loathing for his very existence. She had always known that he was George's child but it had been an unspoken agreement that it was not discussed in her hearing. It was even likely that George had forgotten the incident and had no inkling of his presence in Sarah's house.

Louise had brushed the boy aside roughly and stormed into Sarah's sitting-room to demand that Cathryn

Manners and her child should be sent away immediately.

Impatient with Louise's lack of charity and stupidity, Sarah could understand the mental distress. Reluctantly she promised to ensure that Cathryn left London. Thomas told her that it had been bound to happen: that it was amazingly fortunate that Louise had never met the boy before. Sarah retorted sharply that fortune had nothing to do with it: it had been her skilful management alone which guaranteed that Cathryn and Daniel were out of the way whenever Louise or her children came to the house.

Sending Cathryn into the country was yet one more thing that Sarah lived to regret. She had lost a friend and companion and housekeeper: she sorely missed the boy who had been almost as dear as though he were her own son; Frances had lost a friend and playmate and could not understand why he had been sent away. And within a matter of weeks Cathryn had left The Meads, taking the boy with her, and disappeared. Sarah had tried to trace her without success and now she knew nothing about the woman or her whereabouts. She felt that she had failed Cathryn and it grieved her that Daniel should grow up without the many advantages that she could have given him.

She looked across the room at George with dislike and contempt in her eyes. He was half-dozing in his chair, a tall, big-boned man running to fat, scarcely able to conceal his boredom and obviously impatient for the evening to end.

She wondered, as she frequently did, what had gone wrong in that marriage. Louise was an unhappy and frustrated woman, finding that children did not recompense for the love and comfort of a faithful husband. But it was too late to turn back to George with affection and interest. Her children were the reason for her existence. At thirty-six, she could not regain the youthful adoration — yet she was too young to be reconciled to an unsatisfactory marriage to an indifferent man.

Sarah wondered idly how it would all end. Was George content to go on living with a wife who pushed him into the background, bored and indifferent? He was still of an age to be attractive to women and he retained enough of his former good looks to catch the eye. Louise was unhappy. Was she content to spend the rest of her life with a man who no longer cared for her, had little interest in her doings or in their children and made no secret of his affairs with other women?

The shrilling of the telephone interrupted her thoughts and with a word of excuse to Thomas and Mariana, she crossed the room to lift the receiver. Her conversation was brief and when she turned back into the room it was obvious from her pallor and the glitter of her eyes that she had received bad news.

"I'm sorry but I shall have to go

out," she announced. "Can you enjoy yourselves without me — or do you want to bring the party to an end?" That brief apology was all she would offer for the abrupt departure from her guests and she had no intention of making explanations while George and Louise were present.

Dismayed but used to Sarah's quixotic impulses and correctly assuming that one of her lame dogs was in trouble and needed her help, it was decided that the party should continue while the children were enjoying themselves and Sarah promised to return as soon as she could.

She hurried to her room and changed into a plain navy suit, added a trim little hat to match, and left the house to hail a passing taxi.

It was a matter of a few moments to the hospital on Hyde Park Corner and she talked to the sister in charge of the ward before making her way to the white-covered bed.

She was shocked by the change in

Cathryn but she had long since learned to school her expressions and there was no more than warm concern in her eyes and voice as she bent over the sick woman.

"I'm so glad you sent for me, Cathryn," she said gently. "I've been worried about you."

Her dark eyes burned like black coals in the pallid face and her thinness caught at Sarah's heart. "I knew you'd come," Cathryn said weakly. "You're the only friend I've ever had."

Sarah drew up a chair. Compassion touched her lovely face as she looked at Cathryn for she had been told that there was no hope and that she was not expected to live above a few days. She had neglected herself and her health for too many years and now she was paying the penalty.

"What have you been doing?" she asked quietly. "Where have you been living? Why haven't you been in touch with me before?"

Cathryn turned away her head. "You

did so much for me," she murmured. "It was time I stood on my own feet. And Daniel was my child ... not yours." There was a faint resentment in the words that hurt Sarah unexpectedly. Colour stormed to her cheeks. Had it seemed that she was trying to wean Daniel from his mother? Had Cathryn really felt that she no longer had any say in Daniel's upbringing and future? And was this really the reason for her disappearance?

She refrained from pointing out that it did not seem as though Cathryn had made a very good job of standing on her own feet.

"How is Daniel?" she asked.

"All right. That's what I wanted to see you about. I'm dying, Sarah — and I want to know that he'll be all right."

Sarah touched the thin hand gently. "I'll look after him, Cathryn ... you can be sure of that."

"You ... love him, don't you?"

"Very much," she said quietly. "He

won't want for anything, I promise you."

"I wanted to do so much for him . . . and I haven't been able to do anything. There hasn't been the money or the time. Did they tell you what happened?"

Sarah nodded. "Yes . . . I only wish I had known that you were in trouble, my dear."

"It doesn't pay to be proud," Cathryn said bitterly. "I should have allowed you to go on supporting me and the boy. I should have continued to sponge on you for as long as I could. It didn't do me any good uprooting myself and trying to earn a living by taking in lodgers. If I couldn't take any more of your charity I should have thought about the boy. He's been running wild — and I haven't had the time to see to him . . ."

Sister came up to the bed and laid a quiet yet compelling hand on Sarah's shoulder. "I'm sorry, my dear . . . but I think that's long enough."

248

Sarah rose obediently. "I'll come again tomorrow, Cathryn," she said. "But where can I find Daniel? I must take him home tonight." She used the word 'home' quite unconsciously and did not know the jealousy which burned in the sick woman's breast at her words. Cathryn had always feared that Sarah Fallow's love for Daniel would become too embracing, too possessive — and she had always resented the young woman's manner of speaking and behaving as though Daniel was entirely her responsibility and, at times, entirely her child.

Reluctantly, because she had no choice, she gave the address and added: "You'll be lucky if he's there. He's usually roaming the streets with the other boys, getting up to all kind of mischief, I don't doubt."

"I shall find him," Sarah said firmly. "Now, there isn't any need for you to worry any more, Cathryn. Is there anything I can bring you tomorrow?"

"A shroud," she said bitterly and

turned her face away from Sarah.

She stood irresolute for the briefest of moments then, at a nod from the sister, she walked away from the bed. Her thoughts were in a turmoil. The story she had been told was sordid and difficult for a woman like Sarah, sheltered and cherished all her life, to credit. She had felt a swift admiration for the woman who had found her independence and determined to earn enough to keep herself and her son by taking in lodgers in the small house she had managed to rent. She had been horrified to learn that one of the lodgers had returned home late at night, drunk and disorderly, and when rebuked by Cathryn, had turned on her savagely. Daniel had leaped to her defence and been felled to the ground with one blow from the big man's hand. Cathryn had seized a poker and revenged her son and the attack on herself but the man had snatched it from her hand and beaten her unconscious before leaving the house. The police, called by another lodger, had not as yet traced the man. Cathryn had been admitted to hospital, not seriously injured, and a thorough examination had shown that she was in the last stages of lung cancer. The shock of the attack had caused her to deteriorate rapidly and now there was little hope of her living more than a few days.

Cathryn was still a young woman and Sarah was grieved and shocked by the knowledge of her fatal illness. But she was more concerned at this moment for the youthful Daniel, made more anxious by Cathryn's comments, and pained by the admission that he was 'running wild'.

Another taxi took her across London and into a poor part of the city where the small, meagre houses huddled close together in squalid streets and where the signs of neglect in the children who played in the gutter caused Sarah's tender heart to ache.

She found the house with some

difficulty and knocked in vain at the door. A thin, slatternly woman came to the door of the next house.

"She's in 'orspital," she said, studying Sarah with blatant curiosity.

"Yes, I know. Do you know where I might find her son?"

The woman shrugged. "'E might be anywhere. Out on the streets, 'e is, all day and 'alf the night. She don't bother with 'im much . . . can't blame the kids if they go wrong if the mothers don't keep an eye to 'em, can you? You a relative of 'ers?"

"Er . . . not exactly," Sarah said and there was a certain coolness in her voice which should have put the woman in her place.

"Thought you weren't. She don't look the type to have fancy relations . . . although she's a dark 'orse, that one." She looked Sarah up and down with increased interest. "You the Probation Orficer?"

Sarah stared at her. "No! Daniel isn't in that kind of trouble, is he?"

She shrugged. "Wouldn't be surprised, I wouldn't. Kids run loose all day — what yer expect? You talks like a Probation Orficer. From the school, are you? I warned 'im they'd be after 'im if he kept playing truant."

Sarah felt that she had had a surfeit of this woman's impudent curiosity. Yet she did not want to alienate her if it was possible that she did know where Daniel might be.

"Who has been looking after him while his mother is in hospital?" she asked politely.

"Well . . . me, after a fashion, I suppose. I gives 'im his meals when he bothers to come for 'em and I keep 'is clothes clean when I can get 'im to change 'em. Don't see much of 'im, reely. A lone wolf that boy is. Why?" There was sudden antagonism in her voice. "Who's been complaining?"

"I'm a friend of his mother. I've come to take Daniel home with me. You see, I've only just heard that Miss . . . Mrs. Manners is ill and I've been to see her. She's asked me to take care of her son."

The woman gave her a hard scrutiny. Then she nodded and threw open her door. "That's different. He's 'ere. 'aving 'is supper. Danny!" She raised her voice in a raucous shout. "Come 'ere, willyer? There's a lady wants yer!"

The boy came out of the kitchen, tall, outgrowing the long trousers and ragged blue jersey, a slice of bread and jam in his hand and the stickiness around his mouth confirming that he was indeed having his 'supper'.

"Who is it?" he asked resentfully. Then he saw Sarah and met her smile and the compassion in her eyes. He sniffed and ran a dirty hand across his mouth. "Oh, it's you," he said ungraciously.

She held out a hand to him. "How are you, Daniel?"

He reddened and looked at the neighbour with some embarrassment, sensitive to the wealth of difference between the two women which was emphasized to him by Sarah's cultured voice and elegant clothes. "I'm all right. Have you seen my Mum?"

"Yes, I have. I went to see her this evening and I've promised her that you shall come back to live with me and Frances. Will you get your things, Daniel?"

He scuffled his feet awkwardly. "Don't know that I want to go . . . " He looked down at the floor.

Sarah was taken aback. He could not wish to stay in these surroundings, dependent on the unreliable generosity and kindliness of neighbours. She said firmly: "I'm afraid you haven't any choice, Daniel. Get your things . . . I've a taxi waiting and it's getting late."

Her tone brooked no disobedience and Daniel was accustomed to obeying, albeit reluctantly, the note of authority in the voices of policemen, schoolteachers and welfare officers. Within a few minutes he was ready, carrying a small attache case that contained all his worldly possessions and with a scruffy, excitable terrier or what passed as such beneath his arm.

"Is that your dog?" Sarah asked, dismayed by his appearance and yet too kind-hearted to part him from his dog when it must seem that he was leaving everything to which he was accustomed.

He nodded. "Scruff," he announced proudly. He held the dog towards Sarah. "Shake hands, Scruff." The dog barked and extended a paw trustingly, his limpid brown eyes full of friendliness. Sarah could not suppress a smile and she obediently clasped the dog's paw for a brief moment. She turned to thank the neighbour for looking after Daniel since his mother had been in hospital although she privately thought that little care had been lavished on the boy who looked dirty and ill-fed. The woman received the thanks with an ungracious sniff but her eyes and reluctant smile brightened as Sarah thrust a five pound note into her hand, caught Daniel by the shoulder and hurried him out to the waiting taxi . . .

She was relieved to find that her guests had departed and she wasted no time in sending Daniel to have a bath and giving instructions that a room should be prepared for him.

When he had gone to bed, shy and ill at ease in the surroundings which had once been so familiar but which now seemed alien to him, Sarah relaxed with a glass of sherry and a cigarette. The house seemed quiet and still after the merrymaking of the day and she was abruptly aware of a feeling of loneliness.

She heard the peal of the doorbell and wondered who could be calling at this late hour. Then a familiar voice in the hall, speaking to Tyler, brought swift colour to her cheeks and a catch to her heart.

The door opened. "Don't worry . . . I'll announce myself," Martin said easily and then he was crossing the room towards her with a smile.

"Why, Martin! I didn't expect to see you! I thought you were in Italy," she said, struggling with the words, determined not to betray how very much his visit meant to her.

"I came back unexpectedly," he told her. "I thought I'd drop in to wish you a Happy New Year."

"It's lovely to see you," she said as calmly as she could. "You'll have a drink? A cigarette?" She walked to the decanters and poured him the whisky and water he always enjoyed.

"I'm too late for the party, I see," he said, looking about the empty room with a faint smile.

"It rather petered out," she said ruefully. "I had to go out." She gave him his drink and resumed her seat, looking up at him with no more than warm friendliness and interest in her eyes. She could not reveal more of the hurtful emotion that swept through her for she knew it would not be welcome. He had made that very clear during the intervening years since Giana's death. He had never forgiven her for treating his love and his proposal of marriage so lightly . . . never forgiven that flimsy fabrication of an engagement to another man . . . and she could not tell him the truth nor make it obvious that she would gladly welcome his love and the chance of marrying him if it ever came her way again.

They were ill at ease with each other . . . perhaps because it was the first time they had been alone with each other since the day she had told him of her intention to marry Alan Fitzgerald. They had never met since without one or more of the family being present — and she wondered why he had sought her out this evening. Because he had expected to find the house full of her guests? Or because he had hoped to find her alone . . . and her heart leaped with hope at the thought.

She rushed into speech, began to tell him about Cathryn and her illness, the incident with her lodger, the boy

Daniel. He listened in silence — a silence that she could not determine to be approving or otherwise.

"I can't help blaming myself," Sarah said ruefully. "I sent her away . . . when she was happy and secure! I was her only friend and I let her down."

"You wanted to be her friend and I admit that you were very good to her . . . but you didn't help her in any way," he said quietly.

She stared at him. "What do you mean?"

"Cathryn Manners wasn't the type to appreciate all you did for her, Sarah. She wasn't grateful for a good home, for your kindness, for your concern. She disliked you and took all you gave, resenting the need to take it. She was jealous of your interest in Daniel. You sent her away from here — and that was her opportunity to escape your kindness and concern and to ensure that your connection with Daniel was severed. Your motive was good — but your method was wrong,

I'm afraid. You encouraged her to keep the child she never wanted and never loved . . . and although you were willing to bring Daniel up as your own son and she didn't want him, she was determined never to hand him over to you! If you had placed her in one of those excellent homes for unmarried mothers, persuaded her to have the child adopted and then helped her to find another job, she would have been grateful and thankful — and independent again. But you did more . . . too much — and she never thanked you for it. Now, she's dying — and she's handing the boy over to you because she knows that she can't do anything for him and because she knows that you will provide him with a good education and an assured future. Not because she's fond of you or grateful to you — or thinks of you as a friend! She is using you, Sarah — as you used her when you wanted to do good, when you needed to feel that you were doing something useful, when you longed for a child of your own and was grateful for Daniel to fill the need."

She stared at him, shocked and dismayed. "You really believe that, don't you?"

"Because it's the truth," he said calmly.

"The truth as you see it!" she flared, angry.

"As anyone but you can see it, my dear. I don't mean to hurt you . . . I just want to open your eyes. Don't go through life believing that people are grateful when you help them . . . they resent being in need of that help and they resent you for being in a position to offer it. If you accept that and continue to help, then that's admirable. But don't do it because you want to be loved and admired and respected — or because you're a lonely woman in need of a husband and a home and children to take up your energies and provide an interest."

She was pale and stricken, realizing

the innate truth of his words — and dismayed by the realization. All her life she had sought to help the lesser fortunate — and only now did she know the real reason for her willingness to do so. All her life she had been desperately in need of love, desperately seeking to feel necessary to someone or something. She had always been loved but it had never been enough to be loved by family and friends. She had to know the love of complete strangers, of all the world. She had to know a reason for living. She had been obsessed with the desire to do something worthwhile with her life — all the time aware that the only thing worthwhile in her estimation was to marry the man she loved and have a family of her very own.

He moved towards her and touched her shoulder. It was the first time he had touched her in years and her hand instinctively moved up to clasp his fingers. "I've hurt you," he said quietly. "Perhaps I've been too blunt."

"No . . . " she said. "No, Martin. You've told me something that I needed to know." She was suddenly angry. "This is entirely George's fault . . . everything! If only he'd left Cathryn alone! I'm very tempted to tell him the whole story — and also tell him what I think of him!"

Martin smiled. "That isn't worthy of you, Sarah. It takes two to make a bargain, you know — and Cathryn must take the blame for some of it. You always thought well of her, I know . . . but the truth is that she was a scheming, sly young woman who hoped to ensure a lifelong maintenance for herself and her child. Unfortunately, things didn't pan out as she had hoped. George ignored the whole story . . . and you stepped in to provide a roof for her head, regular meals and even money in her pocket. That didn't really suit her book at all — but as she couldn't get maintenance from George she was willing enough to take it from you. Speak to George if you must . . . but nothing can be gained by embarrassing him or alienating him. We aren't set up to judge our fellow beings, Sarah. Your main concern must be for Daniel — if you really want to take the boy under your wing."

"Of course I do," she said hotly. "You may be right about Cathryn . . . although I find it hard to believe! — but Daniel isn't to blame for his existence and someone has to care about him!"

He smiled at her with more affection in his gaze than she had seen for longer than she cared to remember. "You really are a golden girl, Sarah," he said quietly.

Again the swift colour flooded her face. She had never expected to hear that teasing endearment again from his lips. She forced a little laugh. "Oh, I must be getting a little tarnished with age by now," she said lightly.

"Gold doesn't tarnish," he told her. He lifted her face with a hand beneath her chin. "Sarah . . . " He broke off abruptly as she averted her face and rose to her feet, struggling for self-control, terrified that she would turn to him, cling to him, sob out her need of him — a need which she knew with all the deadness of her heart that was no longer reciprocated.

"You were saying," she said carelessly as she helped herself to a cigarette and offered the box to him.

He had regained his composure, thankful that her careless movement had checked the impulsive words, thankful that she had spared him further humiliation when he had been so near to speaking of his love, his need of her, his urgent desire to make her his wife. Perhaps she had sensed the words that trembled on his lips . . . and in order to spare him that humiliation had risen to her feet and sought an excuse for the movement.

He smiled — but the warmth and tenderness was lacking in his eyes. "I was about to suggest that we go out and get some dinner . . . and perhaps dance a little," he said easily.

"Yes, I'd love that," she assured him smoothly . . .

She knew that she would cherish the memory of that night when they had seemed to regain the old footing of friends and companions — if not the lovers that her heart wanted them to be. He was courteous, attentive, amusing, interesting and ensured her enjoyment in every possible way. And Sarah was gay and lively with a feverish gaiety, an insistence on the light relationship between them, an emphasis that disturbed her listener on the bewildering whirl of her social life and her popularity with the many men in her life. She did not know that every word, every gesture, seemed yet one more stone on the grave of his hopes and dreams . . .

When he left her at the house in Belgrave Square and made his way back to his hotel, he knew that he would never again give way to the impulse which had urged him to seek her company, to seek some sign that she still cared for him, to seek the merest hint that she might yet be willing to marry him. She could not have made it more clear that she was fond of him in a cousinly or sisterly way, that she was enjoying her life as a gay bachelor girl, that she was in no hurry to marry and settle down — and that if she had ever loved him it was a long time since that emotion had burned brightly in the heart of his golden girl . . .

A few days later, Sarah called on Louise. They talked of trivialities for a few minutes then Sarah came directly to the point as was her way: "I'm afraid you won't like it, Louise, but Daniel's living with me again now."

Louise looked up swiftly from her embroidery. "Why?"

Sarah felt a momentary indignation. She did not have to explain her actions to her sister. But she strove to keep her temper. "His mother has just died and the boy is entirely alone in the world," she said. "I've always been fond of him and I didn't mean to let him struggle through life without friends or family."

The sewing lay idle in Louise's lap and her eyes rested on her sons. "So that woman is dead." Her voice was flat, unemotional.

"Yes . . . I was with her when she died," Sarah told her.

Louise flashed her a glance that was almost contemptuous. "You're so soft, Sarah. Always ready to help the lesser fortunate, aren't you?" And her words held a sneer.

Sarah shrugged. "I've always had so much," she said lightly. "I was fond of Cathryn and I was sorry for her." She stole a glance at her sister's face and found none of the sympathy or pity that she sought, no easing of the grim hatred that Louise had always felt towards Cathryn Manners and her child.

"Sorry! For a woman like that! Her morals were disgusting and she made a fool of you! She should have been on

269

the streets . . . not living in the lap of luxury in your house!"

Before she could stem the words, Sarah said swiftly: "And George? Did you never blame him? Don't you condemn his morals?"

There was a silence and she saw that Louise struggled with her self-control. She studied the coldness of that gentle face . . . and suddenly recalled the gay vivacity, the warmth and sweetness that had been the young Louise's claim to beauty. She looked at the lines which were etched so deeply about her sister's eyes and mouth . . . lines of discontent and disappointment and frustration.

She said quietly: "How unforgiving you are, Louise. You've always known that George was Daniel's father yet you've pretended ignorance all these years, refused to accept the boy's existence, hated his mother and never forgiven George. I doubt if you've spoken about the boy to George . . . or given him the opportunity to admit that he was unfaithful and to beg your pardon . . . "

Though her eyes glittered, her expression was impassive as she broke in: "George isn't the type to admit anything if he can help it. As for speaking to him, don't you think it's a rather delicate subject for a wife to mention to her husband? As for blame . . . you ask me if I blamed George. No, I never have. At first I blamed that woman. Later, I realized that I was more to blame than anyone. I began to cold-shoulder George when Lucy was born. I pushed him into the background and allowed him to stay there all these years. I've denied him everything but talk of the children. I've filled his life with domesticity which bored him to death. I've expected him to put up with everything and go on loving me. Instead we've drifted apart . . . "

Sarah was unexpectedly touched by the quiet recital. "And you? How do you feel about George now?"

"I still love him," she said simply. "But it's too late to change anything.

George has been constantly unfaithful, I know. I pretend that I don't know — and he isn't deceived. He thinks I'm indifferent." She smiled briefly. "We haven't slept together for years. Naturally he turns to other women. So I can only blame myself, can't I? Things might have been different if I'd been different. But it's too late now." She resumed her sewing and her voice was calm and matter of fact as she added quietly: "He wants me to divorce him."

Sarah uttered an exclamation. She was filled with pity for her sister. There was no doubt that she had been an unhappy woman for a long time. George seemed to have no perception — or perhaps years of indifference to his wife's thoughts and feelings had become an ingrained habit.

Only her eyes, dark and despairing, betrayed Louise's inner turmoil and distress as she went on quite calmly: "It's another woman, of course."

"Where is George now?" Sarah

demanded in a tone that hinted that she was ready and willing to do battle with her brother-in-law.

"He's staying at his club, I think. He asked me yesterday if I would divorce him — he said he would supply me with the necessary evidence."

"Do you know the woman?"

"It's that stupid little chit . . . Carolyn Menshaw. She's young enough to be his daughter!" She sighed. "It isn't the first woman . . . you know that! But he's never wanted a divorce before."

"You agreed?"

"Of course not. I have to consider the children, Sarah. I had to refuse!"

Sarah nodded. She scarcely knew what to say. Her sense of justice impelled her to sympathize with George who had known little affection or warmth from Louise during his marriage and who could scarcely be blamed for wanting a young, loving, passionate woman who would make him feel that he was a necessary and vital part of her life. But at the same time she knew compassion for her sister's distress and bewildered realization that her marriage was crumbling about her feet and she appreciated Louise's concern for her children . . .

George Marchmont had felt a little ashamed as he met his wife's stricken eyes. Even to his infatuated senses, it seemed a little ridiculous to consider ending his marriage for the sake of a girl who had been a mere baby when it took place. But Carolyn was young and warm, impetuous and passionate, appealing and lovely — and he overlooked the spoiled, selfish, flirtatious nature, the vanity and greed and extravagance and deceived himself that he could find happiness with this girl who was the epitome of all the things he had hoped to find in Louise. He ignored the slight sense of relief he felt at his wife's definite refusal of a divorce and only thought with some dismay of Carolyn's anger and contempt when she learned of his lack of success.

Carolyn Menshaw was accustomed to getting her own way in everything — and for the time being she wanted George. He was of good family, he was wealthy and influential and he was still a good-looking man with a certain disturbing charm. Defeated in her wish to marry him, she accepted him as a lover . . . and quickly found that money and breeding and good looks could not compensate for the difference in their ages, his reluctance to dance through the night to the dawn and attend the wild parties that she loved, his irritating anxiety for his health and looks — and, more than anything, his obvious concern for his wife and children. While they had been a part of his life, he had taken them for granted, known boredom and indifference. Suddenly cut adrift, he realized that he missed Louise's quiet and easy serenity, the comfort and reassurance of her wifely care, even the domestic details which had so often driven him from the house — and he missed his children. He knew that he had been a fool . . . that he no more loved Carolyn than she loved him. Her youthful impatience and her tendency to flirt with other men hurt him badly. She mocked him for his habits and dress and accused him of being old-fashioned. She laughed at him when he suggested a quiet evening and an early night — and her many extravagances were a constant drain on his resources, for he still had to maintain Louise and the children, pay for the upkeep of the house and for the education of his sons.

Within three months, they had parted . . . the final blow being Carolyn's accusation that he was too old to be a satisfactory lover and that her friends were beginning to sneer at their association.

Hurt and humble, he crept back to Louise and begged her to take him back. He had lost a great deal of his self-possession, his lordly manner and consequential airs. Much to his surprise, Louise welcomed him warmly, told him he had been a fool but she could forgive him and shyly suggested that they should make a new beginning. Thankful, a little touched by her generosity, surprised by her warm ardour which had been denied him for so long and comfortable in the realization that the wife of long standing, the familiar surroundings and the company of his children were very dear to him, after all, he settled down in a way that had never appealed before . . .

Meanwhile, Martin stayed in London and saw more of his golden girl than he had hoped or expected. For she was finding Daniel to be something of a handful and she turned to him again and again for help and advice. He could wish that she would seek him out for a more personal reason but he was glad enough to be available at her call.

Daniel was resenting his lack of freedom. For four years he had known a different way of life and it had been an adventurous, exciting life for a boy with no one to gainsay his movements, to scold or criticize — at least no one to whom he would listen. Now he was bored with having everything made easy for him — and he could not be grateful for a luxurious home, regular and excellent meals, new clothes and shoes, compulsory schooling and many and varied amusements. He disliked Sarah's efforts to correct his grammar and her rebukes when he lied or used bad language — and she tried in vain to appeal to a better nature that might not even exist. He needed a man's firm rein, a man's authority, a man's understanding — and he liked Martin Fallow, liked and trusted him and made every effort to please him.

He missed the rough but affectionate comradeship of the boys who had been members of his 'gang'. Because he was tall and agile, fleet of foot, strong in the arm and quickwitted, he had been the leader of the group of boys who prowled about the slums and swarmed through the street market in search of loot or old junk or stray animals . . . anything which might bring a few shillings to be spent on sweets, cigarettes, visits to the cinema. School had been something to avoid as much as possible: he had preferred the geography of the district in which he lived, the arithmetic of quick bargains in the market and the calculation of gain from their spoils, the history of dashing, swashbuckling films of pirates and soldiers, the language of foul words and vituperative abuse.

It was late one evening when Martin's telephone shrilled. He had been fortunate enough to renew the lease of his old flat in the Albany, the friend who had taken it over from him having plans to live in South Africa, and he had settled down comfortably to his austere, bachelor way of life.

He put aside his book with some reluctance and lifted the receiver. He recognized Sarah's voice immediately.

"I was thinking about you earlier this evening," he told her warmly. It was true. She had been very much in his thoughts for the love that he had believed to be conquered by long absence had been renewed a thousandfold by their frequent meetings of the past few weeks. She was in his blood, a sweet, haunting enchantment, his very reason for living — and with all his heart he wished that she could have loved him, would have married him all those years ago . . .

She disregarded his words. "Martin, can you come? I know it's late . . . but Daniel's run away, I think. I don't know where he is . . . his bed is empty and some of his clothes are gone."

She spoke calmly but he sensed the distress behind the words. "I'll be there in ten minutes," he promised. "Make sure that he isn't anywhere in the house . . . the little devil might be playing a prank on you!"

As he drove through the deserted streets, he thought ruefully of the boy and the trouble he had given since Sarah assumed responsibility for him.

He had been allowed to run wild too long, that was the trouble. His mother had obviously cared little for him and had not worried about him as long as he wasn't under her feet. A boy like Daniel needed a father — or at least some man whose authority he would respect and heed. For all Sarah's willingness to help the boy, to guide him on to the right paths, to remember that the boy was father to the man, she had little or no knowledge of small boys and their thoughts and feelings.

Sarah admitted him to the house herself and he smiled down at her reassuringly, a tall, responsible, reliable man, no longer young although the years had been kind to him.

"I'm so glad you've come," she said thankfully. "He isn't in the house . . . it's been thoroughly searched. I wish I knew why he ran away, Martin."

"You do know, Sarah," he said gently and his eyes held her gaze steadily.

She looked down at her hands. "I'm too possessive?"

"That . . . and other things. You've tried to mould him into something he'll never be, you know. You've tried too hard to banish the boy of the streets and replace him with the boy you want him to be. You must accept Daniel as he is, my dear . . . with more of his mother in his make-up than you care to believe. He wants adventure and excitement. He wants to live for the day and let tomorrow go hang. And, more than anything, he wants to be free and independent and self-sufficient. Feed him, clothe him, educate him by all means . . . but don't dictate his every thought and feeling. He's a boy who wants to run and jump and swing and kick and shout . . . you want him to walk by your side, holding your hand, minding his manners — so that you can claim the credit for making a gentleman out of a guttersnipe!"

She paled. "Oh!"

He smiled. "I'm too frank with you, my dear — and you don't like it these days. Once I could always tell you the truth and you would admit it honestly. Now you believe that you should be hurt and annoyed . . . that I'm trying to humiliate you when I only want to help. Oh, Sarah — my lovely, golden girl . . . don't lie to yourself so much! Know why you do these things . . . know what you want from life and go after it with an honest heart and mind." He caught her hands as he spoke and looked down at her with desperate sincerity and a loving urgency in his eyes.

Sarah was silent, thoughtful. His words had struck home with a force that dismayed and yet brought a warm, hopeful glow to her heart. His lovely, golden girl! Was she still that to him? Did he still care . . . after her rejection of him, after the long and lonely years?

Why had she rejected him? For the first time she delved deeply into that impulsive heart which had denied the love she had always known to be her destiny. Know yourself, he urged . . . know why you do what you do! She had sacrificed their chance of happiness for a quixotic scruple. She had wanted to martyr herself for the sake of a woman who had never put anyone or any scruple before her own desires. She had convinced herself that she had no right to take the opportunity offered by Ann's crime — no right to accept a happiness brought about in such a way. But by what right had she denied Martin his opportunity of love and marriage and children — and didn't he have a right to a true and honest explanation of her unexpected change of heart? She could not have loved him very much, she thought bitterly, unhappily and with greater perception than she had ever granted the subject of her love for Martin. She must have gained greater satisfaction in remaining a spinster for the sake of a scruple than she would have known as

Martin's wife and possibly the mother of his children. Yet she knew that was not true. She had been lonely, unfulfilled, desperately seeking to stifle her need of love with the social work that had always seemed so vital a part of her life.

She had punished them both for another's crime. Martin, innocent of everything but his love for a woman not his wife, had suffered the most, wandering about the world on his own, restless, homeless, loveless.

If she took his advice, went after what she wanted with an honest heart and mind, then she would ask him to marry her. Pride could play no part now in her life. She loved him . . . now she knew how very much she did love him, how empty and futile life was without him, how much she relied on him, how much she trusted and needed him, how much they could give each other in a shared future. Loving Martin and giving him the happiness he deserved and might still desire . . . why had she never before appreciated the importance of these things?

"I understand, Martin," she said quietly. "Thank you."

Her quiet thanks, the look of peace that at last he found in her eyes, brought a surge of tender love to his heart. Was it really possible that he had helped her to a knowledge of what she wanted in life . . . he had been patient for so long, hoping that one day Sarah would waken from her dream of life as she thought it should be to the firm, fine reality. She had always sought the best in people — not in itself a bad thing — but Sarah had never admitted the human failings, the follies and backslidings, the deceits and conceits, the pride and envy and lust and greed. For all her good deeds, her concern for the lesser fortunate, her willingness to help and comfort, Sarah had not loved those she helped because she had not understood them or accepted that they were as worthy of her love as those whose weakness and folly were not so obvious.

He wondered now why she had decided not to marry him. For she *had* loved him . . . more than she had known herself, possibly. Had it been a quixotic impulse . . . a self-deception . . . a conviction that she had been born into this life to bring about the happiness of others and to sacrifice her own personal wishes and desires? He could believe that of his golden girl . . . but he hoped with all his heart that at last she had realized that it was impossible to give happiness to others unless one was a truly happy person, a complete person, with a real love for them that was born of loving and being loved and fulfilling one's destiny.

He reverted to the problem of Daniel. "When did you last see him, Sarah?"

"I sent him to bed . . . about eight o'clock. He went rather reluctantly and after a slight dispute."

Martin smiled faintly. "He still can't settle to a regular bedtime, I suppose."

"No . . . he wanted to watch a

287

television programme that didn't finish until nine but he knew my rules . . . bed at eight o'clock."

Martin produced his cigarette case. "Rules can be bent a little sometimes, Sarah," he said quietly. "He doesn't have to go to school tomorrow, after all — and one late night a week wouldn't hurt him."

"It was my fault," she said wearily. "I allowed him to stay up to see the programme last week . . . naturally he couldn't understand why I insisted that he went to bed this week."

"You must be consistent where children are concerned," he agreed. "Anyway, you say that his bed hasn't been slept in. What did you do after he'd gone up to his room?"

She looked a little shamefaced. "Watched the television programme . . . mean of me, wasn't it?"

"Not really. But I wonder if Daniel knew that you were watching . . . and resented your refusal to let him stay up another hour."

"But surely he wouldn't run away for such a little thing?" she protested.

"Perhaps it was the last of a succession of 'little things'," he suggested. "Daniel is a sensitive boy and you can't expect him to appreciate that all your rules . . . and there have been quite a few, haven't there, Sarah? — are for his eventual good. Possibly he has felt that you were unfair, over-critical — and that he was better off before you gave him a home. You must remember that when he lived with his mother no one bothered very much about him . . . what he did, what time he went to bed, when he changed his clothes, if he went to school, how he spoke and ate. He isn't used to rules and yours must have been a little irksome."

"But I couldn't let him do as he pleased, Martin," she protested.

"Of course not. But I have thought that you could have introduced your rules more gradually and made them a little more elastic. However, the boy has been your concern and I haven't liked to interfere. I've offered advice when it's been sought and I'm glad that you've turned to me for it instead of other people. But Daniel is really too much for you, you know."

"Yes, I know," she admitted ruefully. "And Frances follows his lead so much."

"Why not send the boy away to school? It may be just what he needs."

"He needs a home life . . . a family," she said emphatically.

"Then find a real home for him, Sarah . . . give him a family, a proper family, of his own — or as near as possible. He needs a mother *and* a father — and less luxurious surroundings. He will be in better hands, my dear. If he's as lucky as myself then you need never worry about him again."

She looked at him quickly. "I'd forgotten that you were adopted, Martin. It seems strange to realize all over again that you're not really my cousin."

"Do I seem so cousinly?" he asked

with a faint smile.

The colour touched her cheeks for a brief moment. "No," she said in a low voice. Then she added hastily: "But we were discussing Daniel. I think you must be right. I've tried for three months to make him happy and settled, to make him feel a part of a family — but I've failed somewhere. Perhaps he should go away . . . to a good school or to people who will provide him with the home he needs and a more unselfish love than I can give him." She paused and then went on firmly: "I'm learning, you see, Martin. I know that I want the boy only because, like Frances, he represents the child I've never had. I don't really feel a deep love for him . . . at times I don't think I even like him. He's so . . . secretive, so moody and difficult."

"Isn't Frances?" he reminded her.

"Oh yes! But the relationship is closer — and I've had her since she was a small baby. She believes that I am her mother and she loves me.

I love and understand Frances. I can make allowances for her temperament — but I can't do that for Daniel. I can't love him enough."

"Then you mustn't keep him," he said firmly. "Go on being honest, Sarah. You must consider Daniel and his happiness, his future . . . you'll miss him if he goes but I'm sure you'll soon find another lame dog who needs your help and love and comfort. It might even be me," he added, almost beneath his breath.

She turned to him quickly, her eyes warm and eager. "Martin . . . "

He was suddenly afraid . . . afraid that his foolish words had aroused her compassion and pity rather than a love he would welcome gladly and with open arms. He said abruptly: "Now . . . Daniel. Do you think he might have gone back to the East End?"

She seized on the suggestion. "Why, of course! It's the only place he would go! It was his home for four years . . . he felt that he belonged there!"

"Then we'll take my car and see if we can find him," he said firmly. "Did he have any money?"

She nodded. "My purse is missing," she said sadly.

"Then he isn't walking," he decided. "Any idea what time he might have left the house?"

"No. He went upstairs just after eight and I looked into his room just before I telephoned you . . . about ten o'clock. Standish heard the dog barking about quarter to nine and he isn't in the kennel now . . . so I imagine that Daniel must have collected him and probably the dog was excited at the thought of a walk."

"Oh, Daniel wouldn't have left Scruff behind," Martin agreed with a smile.

They left the house as soon as Sarah had thrown a coat about her shoulders. As they drove away, Martin said quietly: "I suppose you didn't get in touch with the police?"

She shook her head. "Daniel doesn't like policemen," she said simply. "I thought that you would help me to find him and then he could come home as though nothing had happened. It seemed wiser to treat the whole thing as lightly as possible — and not give him the impression that he'd done an exciting, dramatic thing by running away."

"Sensible," he approved. "He certainly wouldn't have thanked you if the police had picked him up and brought him back. As it is, he'll probably be feeling a bit lost and be only too glad to be found by the time we catch up with him."

As they neared the poor, shabby district in the East End of London, Sarah said diffidently: "Will you try the house where he used to live?"

"Good idea. Can you remember the address?"

She told him and they found it after some difficulty for it was a narrow street tucked behind a maze of similar streets and some distance away from the main thoroughfares.

As Martin drove slowly down the street, his headlights picked out the small, huddled figure on the doorstep — and Sarah uttered a cry of relief and thanksgiving.

Daniel was half-asleep but he was brought swiftly to full consciousness by Scruff's excited welcome of the people he recognised as friends. He struggled reluctantly to his feet and threw Sarah a resentful, angry glance. But then he saw Martin and his face was illuminated with a smile that held affection, admiration, respect and relief.

He sat beside Martin on the way back to the house he reluctantly called home and Sarah was silent in the back of the car, listening to his eager questions and half-proud, half-sheepish explanations. She realized how much more Martin could do for the boy than she could . . . and she wondered if Martin would want to keep Daniel and bring him up as their own if she could persuade him that she loved him and needed him and wanted to marry him.

She offered no word of reproach to Daniel that night. As soon as they reached the house, she hurried to prepare hot soup for the child and coffee for herself and Martin.

When she returned, it was obvious that Martin had been having a serious talk with Daniel for the boy was flushed and almost tearful yet a rainbow smile touched his handsome features.

Martin escorted Scruff back to his kennel while Daniel made short work of the hot soup, eyeing Sarah a little doubtfully, very apprehensive and on the defensive as though he expected a scolding at any moment.

Suddenly he put down his spoon, thrust a grubby hand into his trouser pocket and brought out her purse. "Here you are, Aunt Sarah."

She turned quickly. "Oh . . . thank you," she said, a little at a loss.

"I only used enough for the fare," he said. "And for Scruff's. They wouldn't let me take him on a bus so I had to go on the underground — and they made me pay for him."

"Yes, I see," she said quietly.

"I didn't take it for myself," he told her. "I can look after myself . . . but I had to have money to buy Scruff some food in the morning."

She nodded. "Of course."

He inclined his head and studied her thoughtfully. "Were you worried about me? Uncle Martin says you were."

"A little," she said with a half-smile. "I know you can take care of yourself, Daniel . . . but where did you propose to live?"

"With Mrs. Kenny," he said promptly, so promptly she knew that it had been a carefully thought out plan. "She wouldn't have minded. She's got six kids of her own so one more don't make much difference. But I didn't like to knock her up so late . . . I was going to wait till the morning."

"I'm sorry you don't like it here," she told him gently.

He looked down at his plate. "Oh, it's all right, really," he said sheepishly. "It's just . . . well, I'm used to looking after myself, see. I don't like people to go on at me all the time. This is a smashing house and the food's all right . . . but what's the point of having a bath when you're not dirty and changing your clothes before you've hardly worn them and not being allowed to watch the telly when there's something good on . . . "

She interrupted his blunt recital. "We won't discuss it tonight, Daniel. You should be in bed, you know." She spoke kindly but firmly.

He rose from the table and went towards the door. "All right, Aunt Sarah." He paused with his hand on the door knob. "I'm sorry, anyway . . . I should have told you I was going."

She suppressed a smile. Whatever Martin had said to him, it was obvious that some of it had become a little confused. "I understand, Daniel," she said gently. And she did, thanks to Martin and his clear thinking and his direct insight into the truth.

Martin came into the room a few minutes later, having intercepted the boy in the hall and talked to him briefly before sending him to his room with a mock thump on the seat of his trousers. Daniel had laughed with glee and taken the stairs two at a time . . .

Sarah poured the hot coffee. He took his cup with a nod of thanks. "I must be going soon," he said. "It's late and you look tired, my dear." There was no hint in his voice or manner of the longing he felt to take her in his arms and smooth away the weariness about her eyes and mouth with the tenderness of his lips and the comfort of his arms.

She sipped her coffee and looked at him over the cup. Her eyes were very blue and apprehensive, her heart thudding and leaping tumultuously, her trembling hands glad of the cup to hold. "All my life it seems that you've been going away from me," she said unsteadily. "I wish you'd stay, Martin."

He looked at her swiftly, puzzled, disturbed at what seemed an unusual invitation. "You know that's not possible."

She realized that he had misunderstood her impulsive words. She gestured helplessly. "That isn't exactly an invitation to stay the night," she said with a little laugh. "I tried rather badly to let you know how much I wish you would stay with me always."

He set down his cup. "I'm not quite sure what you mean," he said and now his own voice was unsteady.

She bowed her head over her coffee cup. "I think I'd better be as blunt as you like to be, Martin."

He nodded. "By all means."

She placed her cup on the tray by her side. "Will you marry me, Martin?" She was calm and serene, confident of the wisdom of her decision — and wishing she could be as confident of his acceptance of her proposal.

He rose abruptly and walked about the room, his emotions in a turmoil. It could not be possible that Sarah was asking him to marry her! It could not be possible that happiness was within his reach, after all, despite the years of lonely longing and frustration!

Sarah rose, too, and went to him, laying her hand on his arm. "Be still, Martin," she said gently. He turned to her and put his hands on her shoulders and she looked up at him with her heart in her eyes. "I love you," she told him humbly and simply. "I want you to be happy . . . could you be happy with me?"

His hands moved from her shoulders to cradle her golden head with caressing, reverent fingers — and then he drew her to him and kissed her lips, briefly, tenderly and with all the love that possessed him for this lovely, golden girl who had always held him captive. His heart sang a paeon of thankful praise that she had at last realized that the true secret of loving was in giving — gladly and eagerly and joyfully. She had come to him with the offer of her love and a very real concern for his happiness . . . and not her own — although he could believe now that his happiness would mean happiness for Sarah, too.

"I can't be happy without you," he whispered against her lips . . . and she sighed deeply, thankfully, and stood within his strong, protective embrace, her head on his shoulder, and knew that she had found her home, her safe harbour, her anchor on the stormy sea of life . . .

THE END

WITH SOMEBODY ELSE
Theresa Charles

Rosamond sets off for Cornwall with Hugo to meet his family, blissfully unaware of the shocks in store for her.

A SUMMER FOR STRANGERS
Claire Hamilton

Because she had lost her job, her flat and she had no money, Tabitha agreed to pose as Adam's future wife although she believed the scheme to be deceitful and cruel.

VILLA OF SINGING WATER
Angela Petron

The disquieting incidents that occurred at the Vatican and the Colosseum did not trouble Jan at first, but then they became increasingly unpleasant and alarming.

DOCTOR NAPIER'S NURSE
Pauline Ash

When cousins Midge and Derry are entered as probationer nurses on the same day but at different hospitals they agree to exchange identities.

A GIRL LIKE JULIE
Louise Ellis

Caroline absolutely adored Hugh Barrington, but then Julie Crane came into their lives. Julie was the kind of girl who attracts men without even trying.

COUNTRY DOCTOR
Paula Lindsay

When Evan Richmond bought a practice in a remote country village he did not realise that a casual encounter would lead to the loss of his heart.

ENCORE
Helga Moray

Craig and Janet realise that their true happiness lies with each other, but it is only under traumatic circumstances that they can be reunited.

NICOLETTE
Ivy Preston

When Grant Alston came back into her life, Nicolette was faced with a dilemma. Should she follow the path of duty or the path of love?

THE GOLDEN PUMA
Margaret Way

Catherine's time was spent looking after her father's Queensland farm. But what life was there without David, who wasn't interested in her?

HOSPITAL BY THE LAKE
Anne Durham

Nurse Marguerite Ingleby was always ready to become personally involved with her patients, to the despair of Brian Field, the Senior Surgical Registrar, who loved her.

VALLEY OF CONFLICT
David Farrell

Isolated in a hostel in the French Alps, Ann Russell sees her fiancé being seduced by a young girl. Then comes the avalanche that imperils their lives.

NURSE'S CHOICE
Peggy Gaddis

A proposal of marriage from the incredibly handsome and wealthy Reagan was enough to upset any girl — and Brooke Martin was no exception.

A DANGEROUS MAN
Anne Goring

Photographer Polly Burton was on safari in Mombasa when she met enigmatic Leon Hammond. But unpredictability was the name of the game where Leon was concerned.

PRECIOUS INHERITANCE
Joan Moules

Karen's new life working for an authoress took her from Sussex to a foreign airstrip and a kidnapping; to a real life adventure as gripping as any in the books she typed.

VISION OF LOVE
Grace Richmond

When Kathy takes over the rundown country kennels she finds Alec Stinton, a local vet, very helpful. But their friendship arouses bitter jealousy and a tragedy seems inevitable.

CRUSADING NURSE
Jane Converse

It was handsome Dr. Corbett who opened Nurse Susan Leighton's eyes and who set her off on a lonely crusade against some powerful enemies and a shattering struggle against the man she loved.

WILD ENCHANTMENT
Christina Green

Rowan's agreeable new boss had a dream of creating a famous perfume using her precious Silverstar, but Rowan's plans were very different.

DESERT ROMANCE
Irene Ord

Sally agrees to take her sister Pam's place as La Chartreuse the dancer, but she finds out there is more to it than dyeing her hair red and looking like her sister.

HEART OF ICE
Marie Sidney

How was January to know that not only would the warmth of the Swiss people thaw out her frozen heart, but that she too would play her part in helping someone to live again?

LUCKY IN LOVE
Margaret Wood

Companion-secretary to wealthy gambler Laura Duxford, who lived in Monaco, seemed to Melanie a fabulous job. Especially as Melanie had already lost her heart to Laura's son, Julian.

NURSE TO PRINCESS JASMINE
Lilian Woodward

Nick's surgeon brother, Tom, performs an operation on an Arabian princess, and she invites Tom, Nick and his fiancé to Omander, where a web of deceit and intrigue closes about them.

THE WAYWARD HEART
Eileen Barry

Disaster-prone Katherine's nickname was "Kate Calamity", but her boss went too far with an outrageous proposal, which because of her latest disaster, she could not refuse.

FOUR WEEKS IN WINTER
Jane Donnelly

Tessa wasn't looking forward to meeting Paul Mellor again — she had made a fool of herself over him once before. But was Orme Jared's solution to her problem likely to be the right one?

SURGERY BY THE SEA
Sheila Douglas

Medical student Meg hadn't really wanted to go and work with a G.P. on the Welsh coast although the job had its compensations. But Owen Roberts was certainly not one of them!

HEAVEN IS HIGH
Anne Hampson

The new heir to the Manor of Marbeck had been found. But it was rather unfortunate that when he arrived unexpectedly he found an uninvited guest, complete with stetson and high boots.

LOVE WILL COME
Sarah Devon

June Baker's boss was not really her idea of her ideal man, but when she went from third typist to boss's secretary overnight she began to change her mind.

ESCAPE TO ROMANCE
Kay Winchester

Oliver and Jean first met on Swale Island. They were both trying to begin their lives afresh, but neither had bargained for complications from the past.

CASTLE IN THE SUN
Cora Mayne

Emma's invalid sister, Kym, needed a warm climate, and Emma jumped at the chance of a job on a Mediterranean island. But Emma soon finds that intrigues and hazards lurk on the sunlit isle.

BEWARE OF LOVE
Kay Winchester

Carol Brampton resumes her nursing career when her family is killed in a car accident. With Dr. Patrick Farrell she begins to pick up the pieces of her life, but is bitterly hurt when insinuations are made about her to Patrick.

DARLING REBEL
Sarah Devon

When Jason Farradale's secretary met with an accident, her glamorous stand-in was quite unable to deal with one problem in particular.

THE PRICE OF PARADISE
Jane Arbor

It was a shock to Fern to meet her estranged husband on an island in the middle of the Indian Ocean, but to discover that her father had engineered it puzzled Fern. What did he hope to achieve?

DOCTOR IN PLASTER
Lisa Cooper

When Dr. Scott Sutcliffe is injured, Nurse Caroline Hurst has to cope with a very demanding private case. But when she realises her exasperating patient has stolen her heart, how can Caroline possibly stay?

A TOUCH OF HONEY
Lucy Gillen

Before she took the job as secretary to author Robert Dean, Cadie had heard how charming he was, but that wasn't her first impression at all.